BARRELLING FORWARD

BARRELLING FORWARD

STORIES

EVA CROCKER

Published in Canada in 2017 by House of Anansi Press Inc.
www.houseofanansi.com

House of Anansi Press is committed to protecting our natural environment.

21 20 19 18 17   1 2 3 4 5

Library and Archives Canada Cataloguing in Publication

Crocker, Eva, author
Barrelling forward / Eva Crocker.

Short stories.
Issued in print and electronic formats.
ISBN 978-1-4870-0143-8 (paperback). —ISBN 978-1-4870-0144-5 (html)

I. Title.

PS8605.R62B37 2017   C813'.6   C2016-901821-0
                        C2016-901822-9

Cover and text design: Alysia Shewchuk
Painting by Amelia Spedaliere

**Canada Council
for the Arts**   **Conseil des Arts
du Canada**

ONTARIO ARTS COUNCIL
CONSEIL DES ARTS DE L'ONTARIO
an Ontario government agency
un organisme du gouvernement de l'Ontario

*We acknowledge for their financial support of our publishing program
the Canada Council for the Arts, the Ontario Arts Council, and the Government of Canada
through the Canada Book Fund.*

For Mom & Dad

Table of Contents

Dealing with Infestation

THERE WAS A semi-finished apartment below the place Francis was renting and it sucked all the warmth out of his home. The cold made his sheets and pillowcases feel wet; each night he clenched his teeth as he slid his hand into the frigid space between his pillow and the mattress. The toilet seat was freezing. When he used the dryer the downstairs porch filled with steam that froze on the walls. The house had once been attached on both sides but the summer before he moved in, the house to the right got torn down. Now there was only Tyvek separating the side of his apartment from the elements.

He took the place because he loved the high ceilings and the thick, murky glass in the old windows. It turned out the high ceilings meant that even when the radiators were up all the way you had to wear a heavy sweater to be comfortable.

The teaching job was a step in the direction of paying

off his student loans and he rewarded himself by living alone. Before he moved he was living in a basement apartment on Cornwall Avenue with a guy he barely interacted with. If one of them was getting in the shower he'd ask if the other needed to use the bathroom first. That was their whole relationship. The basement apartment had been furnished and warm and affordable and depressing as fuck.

The night he moved into this new place he corrected a stack of tests on photosynthesis with fingerless gloves and three pairs of socks on. He drew check marks next to sloppy arrows travelling from suns with John Lennon glasses to floppy daisies or miniature trees — pairs of out-turned legs with a cotton ball growing on top of them. That first night he believed the chill was because the place had been empty for six months. He turned the heat on low in every room and was reassured by the smell of dust burning on the radiators.

The itching started on his third night in the apartment. He was in his bedroom, dragging his bed away from the draft coming through the wall on the Tyvek side of the house. He noticed a feeling, like needles were being poked into the crook of his elbow and tugged out again. The next night he noticed the itch behind his knees when he was drying off after a shower. Being in the shower was a fleeting relief from the cold, but getting out ruined it. He scratched hard behind one knee and then the other. Mushy dead skin got caught beneath his fingernails.

By the time he went to the doctor there were swollen

scratch marks on the soft skin behind his knees, in his armpits, and between his fingers. Clusters of skinny, brown, zigzag-shaped scabs. The doctor gave Francis a cream to smear on the affected areas. Anti-fungal on the first visit, Cortisol when that didn't work. The coolness of the cream was soothing when he applied it but as soon as it dried the itch reared again. Between the itching and the cold he was barely sleeping. The doctor asked him to think harder about if he was using a new laundry detergent or moisturizer.

He looked forward to work because it was a break from the cold. He felt that his students were beginning to like him. He told one group about a camping trip in Torbay where he and a friend got drunk and accidentally floated downriver and into the middle of a pond on an inflatable mattress. He sometimes showed a funny YouTube video at the beginning of class: a bewildered child babbling after dental surgery, a sleeping dog yelping with its legs jogging while it lay flat on its side. Or if he came across an interesting tidbit about a new development in science he tried sharing that with them. He was surprised by how receptive they were. They loved hearing about the Hadron Collider.

He was the youngest teacher on staff. There were a few women close to his age but he was the only man under forty. He assumed that made him more relatable. He never yelled, because he was afraid of seeming foolish.

Once he looked through the small window in the door of Gordon French's math class and saw Gordon stamping a foot in front of the students. In the back corner a few students were hunched with the necks of their sweaters resting on their noses. Sniggering.

Francis desperately did not want to be the subject of sniggering. He never said anything about texting if it was happening discreetly under a desk. He never refused anyone a trip to the bathroom, even during a test.

PATRICIA TAUGHT GYM on the first floor and his science class was on the third but sometimes they crossed paths in the morning. They'd been introduced at a staff meeting.

Today they were in the teachers' lounge for lunch at the same time. Patricia had a Mason jar with a layered salad. The dressing was in the bottom; she flipped the jar and shook it before dumping it into a shallow bowl from the cupboard.

Francis sometimes brought pasta with pesto and broccoli in a Tupperware container, or a nice sandwich with Dijon mustard and ham wrapped in tinfoil. But today he had a pizza pocket. The plate was already doing its last slow rotation in the lit-up window of the microwave when Patricia arrived.

"I usually pack myself a nice lunch but I was feeling lazy today," he said when the microwave beeped. He pressed the button and the door sprang open.

"Pizza pocket, classic." Patricia was wearing calf-length basketball shorts and a sweatshirt with the school's logo on it. Francis noticed a scar in her eyebrow and a pinprick below her lip where she'd had piercings. She had a tom-boyish, surfer-girl vibe and Francis wondered if she might be a lesbian.

"I usually have pasta or I bring some leftovers to heat up," he said.

"No shame." Patricia leaned against the counter eating her salad. It was almost impossible to eat the pizza pocket in a way that didn't let the sleeves of his shirt flop halfway down his forearm and show his rash from scratching in his sleep. It had been raw and red for almost three weeks. He was self-conscious about it and had started holding his cuffs over his knuckles in public. It was something he would catch himself doing.

They heard the smack of a person being shoved into a locker. Patricia opened the door and took a wide stance in the hallway. This was the type of incident Francis avoided if he wasn't on lunch duty.

"What's going on here?" She was still holding the bowl of salad. The hallway froze. "Someone want to tell me what's going on here?"

Francis stood behind her, in the doorway. He was holding his pizza pocket wrapped in a cocktail napkin from a stack he'd found next to the coffee maker. A drip of sauce was making its way down the back of his hand. He licked the sauce off his wrist and was pretty sure no one saw.

"I dropped some stuff." A girl was on her knees stuffing a mess of papers into her knapsack. A crowd of girls in oversized hoodies and tight jeans had been standing just behind her when Patricia first burst out of the teachers' lounge. Now they began shuffling down the hallway.

"Nobody is going anywhere; I want to know what that noise was." Patricia lifted a forkful of leaves that glistened with salad dressing.

The girls slumped and sighed.

"I've got another forty minutes before I need to be back in the gym. We can stand here for your whole lunch break if you want." Patricia took a bite of her salad.

Francis could see this was making the crouched girl uncomfortable.

"I tripped," the girl said from the floor. She had intensely curly hair; it was pulled tightly away from her scalp and slicked with gel but it puffed up in a bushy ponytail on the back of her head. Teenagers did not use moderation when it came to gels and sprays. Francis had wondered if his itching might be a response to the fug of cologne and hairspray in the junior high hallways. But the itch always prickled to life when he was at home, usually after he'd gotten into his freezing bed. It suddenly dawned on him that the apartment must be infested with bedbugs. He had heard that they could travel through walls and live for months between floorboards without blood.

"All right, move along all of you, get where you're going." Patricia stepped back into the teachers' lounge and shut the door. She turned to Francis. "Thanks for backing me up there," she said.

Francis nodded, too preoccupied to come up with an appropriate response. He was high on a wave of relief from figuring out the source of the itching—even if it meant that his expensive, almost uninhabitably cold apartment was infested.

FRANCIS FOUND A cheap fumigation company and hired them over the phone. Their web site had advertised that an appraisal was included in the cost of fumigation, and a woman arrived that evening to check for the bugs.

The woman had strawberry blond hair pulled into a high ponytail. She barely had eyebrows. She had on a white plastic jumpsuit that tucked into her boots.

"I'm going to leave these on," she said about her boots. She took a pair of yellow rubber gloves out of the pocket of her jumpsuit and hauled them on, snapping them at the wrist. "I can't risk infecting my next apartment. I have a full roster tonight—four apartments after yours."

"Okay," Francis said.

"What makes you think you have bedbugs?"

"I've been itching ever since I moved in here."

"The last tenants probably left an infestation and the landlord didn't deal with it. If you play your cards right you might be able to get yourself reimbursed for the fumigation. How long've you been here?" The woman ran a finger along the window ledge.

"A little over a month."

"They'll say you brought them in with you. Worth a try though. Pretty sure I just saw one." She dropped onto her hands and knees and bent her elbows to get a good look at the baseboard.

Francis leaned in to see the bug. He was rubbing the rash between his thumb and the outside of his index finger. He stopped himself and held the sleeves of his hoodie against his palm.

"You just missed it," she said. Francis was impressed by how agile she was. "The bedroom's in here?"

He pushed the bedroom door open for her. She lifted his comforter and reached under the mattress to get the sheet off.

"Definitely seeing a lot of evidence here." She snuggled the sheet back over the corner of the mattress. "The great thing about fumigation is that you don't have to dry-clean everything. You just leave everything as is, seal her up and I'll fumigate, furniture and all."

"Thank you for fitting me into your schedule," Francis said.

"Not a problem." She held out a gloved hand to him. When they shook, the latex rubbed his rash in an unpleasant way but her hands were bony and warm and feminine and he enjoyed it.

FRANCIS STAYED WITH his friend Rob during the fumigation. He washed all his clothes at the Laundromat and put them through two dryer cycles. A pocket's worth of quarters. Before going over to Rob's he changed in the Pizza Pizza bathroom, the clothes still warm from the dryer. He stuffed the clothes he'd worn while the laundry was going through into a tall garbage bin with a flapping lid.

He slept on the couch in Rob's living room. He'd left the fumigator a key under the mat in front of his door.

When the alarm on his cell phone went off he had a kink in his neck. The throw pillow that had been under his cheek had a dark mark of drool on it. He'd slept more deeply than he had in weeks because it was so warm in Rob's apartment.

When he arrived at school he saw Patricia standing in front of a group of boys.

"Not on school property," Patricia was saying to a boy with a cigarette.

"Two more puffs," the boy said and exhaled through his nose. His hair was buzzed close to his scalp. He had a small frame; the seams where the sleeves of his hoodie were attached to the shoulders were halfway down his skinny biceps.

"Put it out immediately or get off school property," Patricia said. Francis walked slowly, willing the situation to defuse itself before he arrived.

"Suck my dick." The boy dropped the cigarette on the asphalt and stepped on it.

"What did you say?" Patricia clenched her teeth — Francis saw her jawbone bulge.

He could see there was no way the boy would back down from the dare to repeat himself. There were snow-flakes swirling around Patricia and the small crowd of boys in flat-brim baseball caps.

"I said suck my dick, bitch." The boy shrugged his shoulders and walked away from the school. Out into the cold parking lot in his hoodie.

"You're going to regret that," Patricia said to his back. She wrenched the gym entrance door open.

"You're a cunt," the boy yelled into the parking lot.

"Okay, move along, get to class," Francis said to the boys who were left in the alcove by the gym door. He followed Patricia in.

Patricia had a small cinder-block office in the back corner of the gym. She sat down on a plastic chair in her puffy coat and laid her travel mug on the ground. Francis wasn't sure he should have followed her into the tight space. A rack of basketballs and a milk crate of skipping ropes crowded the room, forcing him to stand with his shins almost touching her knees.

"That was overwhelming." She rested her elbows on her thighs and put her face in her hands.

"You were great." Francis rolled his head in a wide loop, clockwise then counter-clockwise. His neck was tight from sleeping on the couch. The weight of his head tugged the clump of seized muscles and he arched into the pain.

"I let that little shit walk all over me." Patricia straightened up with her palms hiding her face so her elbows hovered by her chest. "No one has ever called me a cunt before."

"He was trying to get you to flip out and you wouldn't take the bait. Stop covering your face."

She took her hands down.

"I'm just embarrassed." She exhaled slowly through her nose; Francis thought she might start to cry but instead she gave him a stiff smile. "I think I just need a moment to myself."

"Oh, totally." Francis started backing out of the office.

"I'm glad you saw it happen though," Patricia said.

WHEN FRANCIS GOT home from school he cracked the windows. He couldn't tell if he was imagining a chemical smell lingering from the fumigation or if it was really there. He made gnocchi from a package with his winter coat on. As the miniature dumplings bobbed to the surface he felt immense relief at the thought of being free from the itch.

He looked Patricia up on Facebook and found her. A lot of teachers didn't have Facebook accounts because they didn't want students looking them up. Her page was private but he could see her profile picture. It showed her standing on the edge of a cliff in the summer. She was wearing hiking gear and her hair was blowing behind her in a wild tangle. He moved the mouse over the "Add" button and his finger seemed to jerk down of its own accord. And then, because he'd already added her and he'd had three beers in an attempt to numb himself to the cold, he sent a message.

Hey,
I was wondering if you wanted to grab something to eat
after school some day this week?

It had been two years since he'd had sex. The longest he'd gone without having sex since he was seventeen. He always jerked off in the shower in the morning and when he got home from work. Sometimes again as he was falling asleep. Those were the best orgasms, when he was almost dreaming. They built more slowly than the ones in the early morning or after school. Sometimes he woke up with the bottom of his T-shirt crusted with cum. That night he spat on his hand and jerked it until he was sore. He was imagining what her breasts might be like, what kissing her might be like. What fucking her standing up against the wall in the teachers' lounge might be like. He pictured Patricia and the fumigator making out in his bed, each of them beckoning him to join in by slowing curling a finger at him. He was very hard but the nervousness of waiting for her to message him back made it impossible to cum.

Just as he was falling asleep, the itch prickled to life again. The feeling of something touching him. The feeling of a slow-moving trail of sweat, a flaking piece of dry skin, a glob of phlegm ungluing itself from his throat. Or bugs. It was in so many places at once. Every warm alcove of his body felt occupied.

NEXT HE HIRED a man named Gary with a dog named The Muscle. Gary's page had come up when Francis first searched for fumigators in the area but Gary didn't actually fumigate; he and The Muscle just confirmed the presence of bedbugs. Francis saw Gary pull up and let The Muscle out of the front seat of his Toyota Corolla. Gary had a tan bomber jacket with a corduroy collar. The Muscle was a beagle. He peed on the corner of Francis's building on the way in.

The Muscle sniffed along the baseboards. His ears flopped as he made his way through the living room to the bedroom.

"Bedroom's in here?" Gary pushed the door open himself. Francis heard Gary's knees crunch as he bent to lift the sheet.

"You've been had." Gary did not tuck the sheet back into place. "Go ahead, Muscle — I'm going to let the dog check it out to be safe, but if you had bugs in here there'd be excrement and specks of blood on your mattress."

"No bedbugs?"

"There's no sign of them — you never had bedbugs. Unless this is a new mattress?"

"Same mattress."

"You've been had."

"I've been itching every night," Francis said.

"There'd be tiny bloodstains here if you had an infestation. You should have called us before you had the fumigator in. See, they have to pay off their equipment, you can't trust them. I hate to say it but if I was you I'd be asking my doctor about scabies."

Francis wondered if he should tip Gary and The Muscle. They had only been there for maybe ten minutes. He ended up tipping twenty dollars. He liked Gary and The Muscle. He liked that they got to drive around all day doing tours of people's apartments. He pictured Gary giving the dog the last bite of his cheeseburger as they drove home at the end of the day.

"What does The Muscle do if there are bedbugs?"

"A little yap." Gary was folding the money up and sliding it into his wallet.

"And he only does it if there's bedbugs?"

"Yup. You've got some draft coming in here." Gary slapped a hand against the wall on the Tyvek side of the house.

FRANCIS CALLED A new doctor's office to make an appointment on his lunch break the next day. He closed the door to the empty classroom and sat at a student's desk as he waited for the receptionist to pick up. When he hung up after booking his appointment, he saw a Facebook notification appear on the screen, a new message from Patricia. She'd just typed it; she was probably a couple floors below him in the gym, or maybe she was sitting in her car in the parking lot.

Sure! Want to get a burrito after work today?

After school they left his car in the parking lot and drove to her place in her car. The car was filthy. There was a grapefruit in the back window that had lost its shape in the sun. The bottom of it was completely flat against the carpeted ledge above the back seat.

Patricia lived by herself with a German shepherd. When they got to her house they had to take it for a walk around the block before they took off their boots and coats. The dog tugged at her but she didn't let it drag her around. He could tell that he would quickly fall in love with her gangly strength. They walked to a small park and she unclipped the dog's leash to let it wander and pee on whatever interested it.

"I am still deeply pissed off with that kid," Patricia said.

"I haven't had to deal with a lot of disobedience yet."

"I'm trying to forget about it. I was thinking we could get burritos at this place down the street and eat them at my house. You can order them and I'll wait outside with the dog."

The burritos came wrapped in silver foil. They ate them on a futon in her living room while they browsed Netflix. Francis founding himself hoping that someday soon (tonight was too much to hope for) she would invite him to sleep over and he could sleep the deep sleep he knew would come from being in a warm bed. Maybe it would be dark and he could take off his shirt without her noticing the scratch marks and rash.

"I called his parents. The father asked me what I did to provoke his son, he just kept insisting his son wouldn't behave that way unprovoked." Patricia made air quotation marks as she said "unprovoked." She tugged a piece of chicken out of her burrito and fed it to the dog.

"What an asshole." Francis couldn't stop thinking

about how visible the flaky red bumps on his hands were. It was actually dim in the living room but the lamp was on his side of the couch. He began slowly sliding away from the light shining out of the bottom of the shade.

"He should have apologized to me. Can you imagine if your son's teacher called to say he told her to suck his dick? I would be fucking mortified." The dog was staring up at Patricia with its tongue flopped out. "Was that too spicy for you, Moira? I'm sorry, puppy."

Francis gradually inched his way out of the lamplight over the course of the pilot episode of *The Good Wife*. Patricia interpreted this as him sidling up to her. Francis could tell by the way their arms were touching; her hand was flat on the cushions, waiting for him to put his hand over it. When the final credits rolled she turned and kissed him on the lips. She lay back on the couch and he crawled on top of her and slid his hands up the back of her shirt. At one point Patricia wiggled out from underneath him and reached up to tug the little chain hanging inside the lampshade. The room went dark except for the TV screen and Francis felt his whole body loosen up.

After they made out for a while Francis helped her gather up the wrappers from the burritos and called a cab. She pecked him on the lips in the front porch after he'd done up his boots.

THERE WERE TWO sagging nets strung across the gym and the kids were playing doubles badminton. Francis didn't have class until ten so he had brought Patricia a coffee three mornings in a row. This morning, rap was thumping through the echoey room from a boom box with an iPod plugged into it. "I let them play their music as long as they behave," she'd told him. "I try to make sure it isn't anything overly offensive. It has to be the radio version, the censored version."

Patricia took her coffee and Francis stuck his hand in the pocket of his jacket. They were planning to go out for dinner that weekend. Francis knew he should be strategizing about how to tell her about the rash but he was hoping to wait until after his doctor's appointment. There was a chance it was a weird food allergy or something else uncontagious. His hope was that the doctor would tell him what food to avoid, or prescribe something that made it go away before there was any need to talk about it.

One of the kids jogged over to a dry-erase board set up on a metal easel next to them. She wiped away a name with the side of her fist and marked another in its place. Francis took in the intricate diagram of the badminton competition.

"Did you come up with this system?" he asked with admiration.

"I'm having him hauled off the hockey team."

"The kid with the cigarette?"

"He refused to apologize. I wasn't getting anywhere with the parents. I spoke with Shortall—he thought it was a good choice. There's a tournament and I don't want to be on a bus all the way to Grand Falls with that little fucker." She was talking quietly as the music blared out of the boom box beside them.

"They're 'not participating.'" Patricia waved discreetly. The gym doubled as an auditorium and there was a stage in the back. Boys in winter coats were sitting in a row on the edge of the stage, swinging their sneakers. "In protest. I told them I'm going to be calling home."

"What did they say?" Just as Francis asked, a girl laid her racket on the floor and ran over to the stage to talk to one of the boys.

"Veronica! Veronica, is your set finished?" Patricia yelled at the girl. Francis was startled by how she made her voice carry across the huge room. "If you're finished, you sit on the bleachers. I don't want to have to call your house too."

The girl walked slowly over to the whiteboard to mark herself into the championship tree. "I was just talking to them," she said. She had crusty blue makeup on her eyelids.

"This isn't socializing class, this is gym class."

"You're such a hard-ass," Francis said, teasing, when the girl walked away.

"You need to grow a pair."

"I hate that expression."

Patricia pressed the power button on the stereo.

"That's it for the music until everyone is ready to co-operate." Patricia's voice boomed through the gym.

"The acoustics in here are wild," Francis said, trying to smother the tension between them.

"I've got to wrap this class up now, Francis. Thank you for the coffee."

FRANCIS LAY NAKED on his bare mattress with the scabies cream smeared all over his body. He'd stripped the bed and brought his sheets to the Laundromat before applying it. The cream came in a toothpaste-shaped tube. He'd squeezed some into the palm of his hand and the paste had spiralled on top of itself like soft-serve ice cream. The doctor had said to make sure to work the cream into all the nooks and crannies: the creases of his groin, his armpits, between his toes. He'd told Francis the bugs like moist, warm places. Hairs were sticking straight up out of goosebumps all over his body but he waited ten minutes for the cream to seep into his skin. When the cream dried he got dressed and went for a walk around the block. He liked to be moving around when he had to have a difficult conversation.

"So I went to the doctor about a rash I have," he told Patricia. It was the first time they'd ever spoken on the phone. "She's pretty sure it's scabies."

"I thought that was something dogs got, like fleas."

"It's contagious, you get it from skin-to-skin contact or from clothes." He was anxious to get all the information out before he lost his nerve. "There's a chance I passed it on to you. You should wash your clothes and bedding."

"Fuck, okay, what is it? It's some kind of rash?"

"It's insects that burrow into your skin. They're mostly

active in the night so if you've been scratching at night . . ."

"What the fuck, Francis? How did you catch it? It's an STI?"

"No! It's more like lice — children and teenagers get it. I probably got it at school, the doctor said it's common for it to get passed around schools."

"I've never had lice." She seemed to be focusing her anger, moving from a blustered outrage to being supremely pissed off at him specifically.

"I'm really sorry, Patricia. I went to a different doctor a while ago and she insisted it was an allergy. Then I thought it was bedbugs, I had a fumigator in and everything. There's a cream you should probably get."

"I haven't been itching."

"It takes four to six weeks to become symptomatic."

"Oh for fuck sakes."

"I thought I should tell you." He was pacing in front of Pizza Pizza. He could see they had three slices left in the case by the cash. The pepperoni was curling into tiny bowls under the lamp.

"Good for you, you deserve a medal. What's the cream called? Do I need a prescription?"

"I'm sorry. Permethrin. You put it all over your body, from the neck down, and leave it on for twenty-four hours. I have it on right now." A man in a jaundice-coloured Carhartt jacket tugged open the Pizza Pizza door. Francis watched as the cashier slowly looked up from a cell phone on the counter and the man pointed to the case.

"How big are these insects?"

"You can't see them. I know, it's disgusting. You might not even have it but you should probably get the cream right away, to be safe. There's still lots left in my tube if you want, I have really strong prescription stuff, or I can get you your own."

"I don't want your scabies cream."

"I just mean so you wouldn't have to go get a prescription and everything."

"Are you home now?" Patricia asked.

"I will be in a minute, I'm just around the corner."

When he got back to the house Patricia's sky blue Ford Festiva was parked at the bottom of the steps up to his apartment. The back seat was folded down and the dog was sleeping in the hatchback.

He knocked on her window and startled her.

"Do you want to come up while I grab it?"

"I've got the dog."

"You can bring Moira in," he offered.

"She really needs to go for a walk."

"I honestly didn't know it was contagious. I'll get the cream."

"Actually, I'm coming up. I have to pee," Patricia said.

He went to his bedroom to get the cream.

"Shortall isn't backing my decision to take Patrick Kennedy off the hockey team anymore," Patricia called to him from the bathroom.

He wiped some crusted cream away from the seam where the cap met the tube.

"Does he know it was about smoking? That you were

enforcing the no-smoking policy?" He slid the tube into its cardboard sleeve and took it into the living room. She had come out of the bathroom and unzipped her jacket. "Why don't you bring the dog in? I'll make some coffee, I have a visitor's permit for the car."

He took the parking permit off the mantel behind him and held it out to her.

"Fine." She took the laminated card and went to get Moira.

They sat at the kitchen table, which was empty except for their mugs and the scabies cream. The dog sat next to Patricia with its head in her lap.

"He says the kid is willing to apologize and the father won't back down and the kid is a talented hockey player who shouldn't be *stifled* because of this incident. Stan, the new guidance counsellor, is siding with them."

"What do you think about that? I mean, if he apologizes sincerely, you wouldn't be happy with that?"

"I'm not taking him to Grand Falls. I'm not spending four hours on a bus with a child who called me a cunt. I'll quit my job. He needs to learn that some things can't be forgiven. I'll go back to school and do something else."

"That's letting him win, don't you think? Letting him run you out of a job?"

"I need you to back me up on this. I'm going to need you to back me up in the staff meeting. To say you think I'm right." She took the cream off the table and put it in her pocket.

ON THE DAY of the staff meeting he met Patricia in the gym with a coffee. Three nights had gone by without itching. It was still cold in his apartment but he had started allowing himself to fantasize about spring. About drinking a coffee in shorts on the fire escape, sleeping with only one blanket covering him and the window open a crack.

The kids were playing soccer-baseball. One at a time they approached the centre of the room and punted a ball at the ceiling. Francis saw that some girls had joined the contingent of boys sitting on the stage at the back of the room, refusing to participate.

"I'll be calling their parents too," Patricia said, seeing him notice.

"Have you been itching?" he asked.

"No — I used the cream just in case though. There's half a tube left if you need it."

"Sure. It's going away but I'll take it just to be safe." A boy in skinny jeans kicked the ball and it flew backward over his head. It hit the floor in front of Francis and bounced about eight feet in the air. Francis caught it on the way down and tossed it back to the boy.

"I'll see you in the meeting," Patricia said.

All day he was distracted by the thought of the staff meeting. He assigned group work, got them to correct each other's quizzes. His rashes were clearing up; the areas they occupied were receding. All he had to do was agree. She would formulate the argument and he just had to endorse it.

He got to the meeting before Patricia. He wanted to

sit next to her, but other teachers arrived and sat on either side of him. The items on the agenda were permission slips, hall passes, and a spike in tardiness. There was a heated argument about policy on hats in class and the fact that the newspaper club and the robotics club had to share the multi-purpose room on Thursdays. He said nothing about these topics.

"Okay, I think that wraps things up, any closing remarks?" Shortall asked, shuffling his papers together.

"I'd like to talk about Patrick Kennedy and the hockey tournament," Patricia said.

"We discussed this, Patricia. He's going to apologize." The principal lifted his bag onto his lap and put his folder in it.

"I'm not happy with that solution. He was incredibly rude to me. I don't think he should be allowed to go on the trip."

The other teachers were getting their things together.

"Patricia, don't you think that apologizing will be a positive learning experience for him?" Stan asked.

"He called me a cunt. I've never been called a cunt by anyone." Patricia's voice was raised. "I don't do favours for people who call me a cunt."

The other teachers had stopped moving.

"I have to agree with Patricia," Valerie, the art teacher, said before Francis could. "'Cunt' is a hateful word. I can barely say it. There needs to be a severe punishment for that."

"Look, they're teenagers, you can't get your back up

every time one of them curses at you. You need a thick
skin in this job," Gordon French said, zipping up his coat.

"Cunt is different," Valerie said.

"Thank you, Valerie." Patricia looked at Francis.

"I agree with Patricia." His voice came out quieter
than he meant it to and he could feel a blush spreading
up his neck.

"This matter is decided, I don't want to waste any more
time on it," the principal said.

"Then find a new gym teacher." Patricia stood up and
yanked her jacket off the back of her chair. She slammed
the door behind her on the way out.

"All very dramatic," Gordon French said.

Francis shuffled out of the room with everyone else.
When he got out to the parking lot her car was already
gone.

He called her that night. He was making packaged
gnocchi again, for the third time that week.

"You didn't speak up. I have nothing to say to you. You
knew it was important to me."

"I did, I said I agreed." He held the phone between his
ear and his shoulder as he dumped the pot into a strainer
in the sink.

"You didn't say it loud enough, you didn't say it until
it was too late."

"Please, Patricia, give me another chance. I'll go speak
to Shortall. I really do think you're right." The steam from
the strained dumplings was making his face wet. His eyes
filmed over with tears.

"I gave you a heads-up before the meeting and every-thing. That was your chance."

After dinner he rubbed the cream into his fading rashes. The skin became shiny and soft. It seemed to glow rosy pink in the places where the bugs had congregated.

Auditioning

WHEN THEY WERE teenagers lots of people told them they could be movie stars. They were slim but not scrawny and they had thick hair. Their teeth were straight and white. But what it really was, was that there were two of them. Not quite exactly alike. Sandra had a freckle on her cheekbone that appeared on Rochelle's chin. Rochelle was taller. But the more substantial difference between them was harder to pin down, all the same parts put together slightly differently.

Their mother got them an agent. He was excited about taking on twins. He told them there was a narrow market open to them but they had an excellent chance of getting every job in that market.

The agent suggested they join a gym.

"You look great right now, you're exactly what people are looking for—but you're at an age where bodies fluctuate and it's a good idea to get used to keeping control of it, if you're planning for a life in the industry." He was saying this to them but he was really talking to their mother, gauging her reaction. "Don't overdo it, just get comfortable with having a fitness routine. I say this to all my teenage clients and I think it's good life advice — get started on taking care of yourselves at a young age and you'll be ahead of the game."

"I completely agree with you. I think fitness is important, there's diabetes in our family." Their mother was holding her purse in her lap with both hands.

"What kind of parts is he talking about anyway?" Sandra asked in the car on the way home.

"We don't know yet, Sandy. I think this is very exciting," their mother said.

"Beer commercials," Sandra said.

"It's not going to be beer commercials. He didn't say that," Rochelle said from the back seat. "Anyway, I'd do a beer commercial."

"It's going to be all slutty beer commercials — you know that, right, Mom?" Sandra made eye contact with her sister in the mirror.

"Take your feet off the dash, Sandra," their mother said.

When they got home their mother's boyfriend, Ian, had made chili. He was setting the utensils out on the table when they got in the door.

"I heated the buns," he told them. It was a braided bun loaf; to take a bun you tugged it off the lumpy golden wreath.

Ian had shaggy hair and was always wearing fisherman's

sweaters. Sandra noticed that since he had started staying over, about three months ago, her mother had been wearing a ratty wool pullover around the house. Usually she wore a rotation of Reitmans cardigans and blazers.

"The agent said the girls should start taking an interest in their fitness," their mother told Ian.

"Hmmm." Ian was ladling chili into cereal bowls. The cereal bowls were deeper than the bowls their mother used for soup.

"Well, I think it's good advice, there's diabetes in our family." Their mother accepted a mound of chili and made noises as if she was getting ready to enjoy it.

"I just wonder about some middle-aged man telling teenagers to work out. I just don't like the sound of that, it's creepy." Ian dished up more chili.

"Well, I appreciate your input." Their mother tore a bun from the wreath. "Girls, I've been thinking you might want to call your dad. He'd probably like to hear about the audition."

"I'm going to Lindsey's after supper and Rochelle has a newspaper-club meeting," Sandra said.

"We have to finish collating tonight, the new issue comes out tomorrow," Rochelle added.

Ian had never met their dad. The girls' parents had been separated since they were small, though everyone got along okay. Sandra and Rochelle had spent the last two Christmases with their dad in Victoria.

Early this December, Ian had driven the girls to the mall because their mother had drunk two glasses of wine at a work party. They'd stopped at his apartment on the way so he could feed his dog. It was four o'clock in the afternoon. The apartment was cold and dark in the early dusk; they all kept their coats on. The dog was asleep with his chin resting on the arm of the couch when they came in. The girls stood in the porch while Ian walked through the kitchen in his boots. He opened the back door and the dog ran out onto the patio.

"I'm just going to let him out for a minute." Ian took a bag of dog food out from under the sink. He filled the dog's water bowl.

"You should leave a light on for him when you go out," Rochelle said from the porch.

"You're right—you should always have the lights on when you're not around. Discourages people from breaking in." Ian flicked a switch and a frosted globe in the centre of the ceiling filled with cloudy yellow light.

"I have to pee really quick." Sandra bent down to undo the slush-coated laces on her hiking boots. The apartment was one level; you could see the door to every room from the porch.

"Did you live here with your old girlfriend?" Sandra heard Rochelle ask. Her voice was very clear; Sandra worried they could hear her peeing through the bathroom door.

"Yup, a long time ago." She could hear Ian putting dishes away, cupboard doors closing.

"Did you guys move in here together?"

"She took all her stuff; this is my stuff."

Sandra flushed the toilet.

"What're you going to do with your stuff if you and Mom move in together?" Rochelle was saying when Sandra opened the bathroom door.

"I don't know. It's not important. Maybe the couch could go in your mom's rec room. I might have some kitchen stuff you guys could use. You don't have a slow cooker, do you?"

"I don't know what a slow cooker is," Rochelle said.

"I do," Sandra said.

"Tell your sister." Ian let the dog in and it shook snow onto the kitchen floor.

THEY FLEW TO Toronto for an audition the agent got them. Their mother was a real estate agent, and she had to re-arrange several viewings to make time for the trip. Sandra and Rochelle were missing at least two days of school. If they made it into the second round of auditions their mother might have to push all their return flights back.

Ian drove them to the airport in their mother's car. He helped carry their bags up to the check-in desk.

On the plane their mother surprised them by ordering a gin and tonic.

"This is an adventure, girls." She twisted in her seat so she was facing Sandra, who was sitting next to an old man in the row behind.

Sandra tried to order a coffee but her mother wouldn't let her, so she and Rochelle both got 7 Up.

The cheapest plane tickets had been for the day of the audition. They checked into the hotel and got dressed in outfits their mother had picked out.

The agent had emailed instructions about appropriate attire for the audition. Their mother had read his email aloud to them in the living room.

"This is a guy who knows the industry, we don't know anything about the industry," she told them.

Ian had been leading the FibreOP guy around their house during this conversation, showing him phone jacks and cupboards to run the wires through. Getting FibreOP was Ian's idea.

"Adult women don't dress alike," Sandra said, as the guy trailed a cord along the perimeter of the living room.

"Lucky neither of you are adult women. Mr. Andrews suggests navy slacks and a white button-down. That'll be nice, very grown-up."

The audition was in a section of a mall that was under construction; huge spaces were roped off with lengths of caution tape. Every few feet there were signs on printer paper Scotch-taped to the wall. They read "Major Talent Casting" and had arrows below them. A coffee kiosk at the edge of a stretch of bald concrete was lit up by construction-site lamps with wire grills over headlight-sized bulbs. Their mother stood in a mess of criss-crossed extension cords in front of the counter and bought cinnamon rolls with icing.

They ate them out of wax-paper sleeves on the escalator. The rolls were dense and sweet. Sandra hadn't expected to feel nervous but she was finding it hard to take a deep breath. It was the same feeling she had when she got up in front of the class to do presentations.

A long line of girls was waiting outside the door of the room where the auditions happened. Some were leaning against the cinder-block wall and some were sitting on their winter coats on the concrete floor. There were many pairs of matching outfits.

"Why don't you girls call your father while you wait? I'm going to go pee." Their mother handed Rochelle her phone.

"Are you going to call?" Sandra asked once their mother was on the escalator with her back to them.

"It would be a distraction. We should focus," Rochelle said.

Sandra nodded. They shuffled ahead in the shrinking line.

"He's probably busy anyway. He's probably at work," Sandra said.

"He's probably out hiking with his girlfriend." Rochelle took a compact out of her pocket and ruffled her hair, tilting the little mirror from side to side.

IT WAS IMPOSSIBLE to tell how the audition went. Their mother waited outside the door while they read from a teleprompter projecting onto the back wall of the room. The commercial was for Tupperware. Three men sat at a fold-out banquet table with a thick plastic top and metal legs. They took notes on clipboards. They asked the girls to jog across the room like they were trying to catch a bus, one at a time and then together. They asked them to say "Thanks, Mom" like they really meant it, again and again.

At the end of the audition Rochelle walked up to the table, smiling like Shirley Temple, before extending her hand to each of the men. Sandra hung back. The new blouse was tight, it puckered open between the buttons.

"Thank you, we've got a lot of girls to see, we'll call you this evening if we're interested in having you audition again." The man at the end of the table got up and pushed the door open for them. As they left he waved in the next set of twins.

After the audition they found their mother over by the escalator, on the phone with Ian.

"Can you check when snow-clearing is? I might need you to move my car...Oh my God, yes, use it whenever you want."

In the hotel, Rochelle and their mother shared a double bed and Sandra slept in a single, closer to the window. At ten thirty their mother's phone started vibrating on the nightstand between the beds. The vibrations made the empty nightstand shudder and they all woke up confused. Their mother sat up and grabbed the phone.

"Hello, yes this is she...yes, we can definitely make it, let me just get a pen so I can take down the address."

Their mother waved her hand and Rochelle got up and dangled her mother's purse by the strap. Their mother batted the purse away and pointed a finger at the hotel stationery and pen, her straight arm bouncing urgently in the air. Rochelle dropped the purse and scrambled for the pen.

"You got a callback! The second audition is Monday morning. I'll have to move our flights."

They spent the next morning walking around the city; their mother found them a pair of dresses to wear to the callback. She took a picture of them with her phone in front of the dressing room doors and texted it to the agent. They wandered around the big store, waiting for the agent to okay the dresses before their mother paid for them.

They walked three abreast on the wide sidewalks. Sandra's hands were freezing. Rochelle was wearing mittens with the outline of Newfoundland knitted into them; their mother had a pair of hairy pink gloves. She kept offering to give Sandra the gloves but Sandra wouldn't take them.

Sandra stopped in front of a narrow store that sold nothing but cell phone cases. There was no window separating the front of the store from the sidewalk. It was very bright and the cases were all shimmery-glimmery with holograms and rhinestones. A girl with baubles in her pigtails stood at an island in the centre of the store wearing a puffy winter coat. Sandra took her hand out of her pocket to run her fingers over the back of a rhinestone case.

Rochelle loved the plastic replicas of sushi in the windows of restaurants. She bought a key chain for a dollar that was a miniature ramen bowl with hard plastic noodles looping in and out of a gel that was tinted yellow to imitate broth.

"Try and think of something we can get for Ian, girls, a little souvenir," their mother told them. They picked out a globe-shaped paper lantern because it was cheap and would fold up and lie flat in a suitcase.

They had supper in a restaurant off the lobby of the hotel. There were squeeze bottles of ketchup on every table and plastic plants on a stubby wall that cut through the dining room. Sandra's hands were still burning from the cold and her fingertips felt as if she had let glue dry on them. The new dresses sat in a bag propped on the chair across the table from her.

In bed that night her hands still hurt from the cold. Whenever Sandra wished for something, she pushed her tongue hard against the roof of her mouth and thought *please* about what she wanted. She was lying with her hands between her thighs looking out the window. She thought *please* that they wouldn't get the commercial. It was about a woman who had six children. Tupperware made getting their lunches ready in the morning a breeze. The girls would be the first of a stream of blond children to snatch a paper bag off a kitchen island on their way out the door.

In the morning Rochelle got the first shower. Sandra and her mother sat on their beds. Her mother's ankles were sticking out of the legs of her slacks; her feet barely reached the floor.

"I know you're not crazy about this, Sandra. A part of

my job as a mother is to make you do things you don't want to do. You have to take advantage of opportunities."

Sandra looked out the window.

"I'm going to go for a walk."

"By yourself?"

"Just around the block, to get a breath of fresh air. I'll be back in ten minutes."

"Fine. You can meet us in the restaurant."

Sandra zipped the key card to the hotel room in the pocket of her parka and jogged down the hall. She jumped as the elevator began to descend and was suspended for an unnaturally long time. One small leap for one twin. Then she landed with extra weight on the carpeted floor. She felt it in her stomach and knees.

People were on their way to work, walking quickly with coffees in their hands. She had almost a hundred dollars in her bank account from her paper route. She had seen a Shoppers Drug Mart down the street from the hotel; she found the stationery aisle and bought a pair of children's scissors with curved blades and chunky plastic handles. On the way back she saw sparks spray off a streetcar cable as metal met metal, and she tilted her head back to let the height of the buildings make her dizzy. She took a deep breath of cold, exhaust-filled air.

Walking back through the lobby, she saw her mother and sister sitting in the restaurant with three menus, and three sets of cutlery rolled in paper napkins. She passed by casually, maybe even more slowly than she normally would. She waited for the elevator along with a family barricaded behind a circle of luggage. A mother, father, and toddler in a snowsuit. She helped them by heaving a suitcase half her height into the elevator, gripping the leather handle with both hands.

It took her three tries of sticking the card into the slit in the door and pulling it back out to get the little mound of green plastic to light up and let her in.

In the mirror she grabbed a handful of her shoulder-length hair. It was hard to get the scissors to shut on the thick wad of hair; she did a series of tiny open-and-shut motions that made her hand ache. Then she was holding a forearm's worth of hair in her fist.

Sandra dropped the hair into the oval-shaped waste-basket by the toilet. She started making little snips, trying to get as close to the scalp as possible. In the end there were places where she could see the white of her scalp and other places where the hair was nearly half an inch long. It wasn't how she'd envisioned it. She needed a buzzer like she'd seen her father use to keep his stubble even.

Sandra walked into the restaurant. There was a board with "Stuffed French Toast Special" and "Please Wait To Be Seated" written on it in dry-erase marker. Rochelle saw her before her mother did.

"What did you do?" her mother said.

They had plates with scrambled eggs and buttered toast, and pinky-finger-sized sausages. Sandra was suddenly very hungry.

"I was proud of you." Their mother was calmly furious.

"I hate you," Rochelle said.

"I can't believe you would do this to your sister. You look like someone with terminal cancer, did you think about that?"

"Sorry."

"What were you thinking? I want to know. What went through your head?" Their mother dropped her knife and fork onto the table. "Do you know how much it cost to move our flights?"

"Lots of people have this haircut — it's just a haircut. They might not care. I could wear a wig."

"You are a very selfish person. I don't know what to say to you. Go up to the room."

Sandra began to walk away, wishing for the French toast special.

"I hate you," Rochelle said again, to her sister's back.

THEY HAD PLANNED to go to the CN Tower in the morning and have lunch with a cousin who had just moved to Toronto. Her mother and sister spent the day without her.

"Do not dream of leaving this hotel," her mother said before closing the door behind her.

Sandra put her bathing suit on under her clothes and wandered around the carpeted hallways until the smell of chlorine led her to the door of the pool. She thought about running away; maybe she could live with her cousin. She used her paper-route money to eat lunch by herself in the restaurant.

At the end of the day Sandra heard her sister and mother outside the hotel room door and got under the covers and pretended to be asleep. She lay on her side facing the window, breathing heavy wet breaths through the comforter while they watched *America's Next Top Model*.

"You'll be going to that audition. Who knows, they might be so impressed by your acting that they use you anyway," their mother told Rochelle.

"They obviously don't want a bald girl in the commercial. The other girls are going to think we're idiots."

"This is what pursuing your dreams is like, Rochelle. It's difficult. There will be obstacles. You know I don't like to speak poorly of your father but he always gave up without a fight and I don't want you adopting that attitude."

Sandra heard her mother tug the sealed mouth of a chip bag apart.

"What about Ian?" Rochelle asked, which was exactly what Sandra wanted to say. Silently, she nosed her face out from under the covers. Looking out the window she could see into an office building across the road. Most of the lights were off, but she could see into a few rooms with cubicles that had carpeted dividers for walls.

"What about him?"

"Do you want me to be like Ian?" Rochelle asked.

"I don't want you to be like anyone. Leave Ian alone."

"Is he moving in with us?" Sandra couldn't believe Rochelle was asking this. Did her mother and sister always talk so openly without her?

"Did he say something about that?"

"No." Sandra was impressed by how casual her sister's voice sounded.

"Well, maybe." Their mother sounded shy.

There was a roar of applause and cheering from the TV.

"I think Marsha will win," Rochelle said. "It's always the underdog. Someone who took bad pictures for the first few weeks."

"You might be right," their mother said.

THE NEW DRESSES were burgundy with three-quarter-length sleeves and a boat neck. They looked like something an eight-year-old would wear to a Christmas party. Rochelle stood in front of the mirror while her mother combed her hair into a French braid. Sandra sat cross-legged on the bed with her knees sticking out of the dress's skirt.

"This is stupid. We look like a circus act. I don't even want to go anymore." Rochelle had been crying and her face was swollen.

"Get me an elastic, Sandra."

Sandra slid off the bed and got an elastic from the counter in the bathroom. She held it out in her palm as her mother drew the bottom of Rochelle's braid together.

"Well, we're just going to show up," their mother said. "We're going to suggest your sister could wear a wig and see what happens." She snapped the elastic around the scrawny end of Rochelle's braid.

"When I was your age I sold sandwiches in my father's store," she said. "I made the sandwiches the night before, three kinds: ham and cheese, egg salad, and BLT. It was a lot of work, frying the bacon and making the egg salad, but I got to keep all the money. What I learned was that the sandwiches had to be made every night. People would come into the store looking for the sandwiches and they had to be there. Even if I had debate club after school or my friends were going to a movie, people were expecting the sandwiches. I'm trying to give you girls a lesson like that. Consistency, responsibility."

"I'm responsible," Rochelle said, patting down the top of her hair.

"Yes, you are," their mother said.

Sandra bent down and laced up her boots so she wouldn't have to look at either of them.

Their mother gave them thirty dollars to get breakfast in the restaurant while she phoned the agent.

"I don't want to sit with her," Rochelle said.

"Rochelle, I don't have time for that. Order me a club with a side of Caesar salad, I'll be down shortly." Their mother was squinting at her phone, rolling through her list of contacts. "Sandra, I hope you know that it's humiliating for me to have to tell Mr. Andrews what you've done."

Sandra didn't say anything until she was alone with her sister in the elevator.

"I said sorry," she said. Rochelle was staring straight ahead at their mismatched reflections in the metal door.

"I'm still mad," Rochelle said. "I'm going to be mad for a

long time, maybe forever, maybe we aren't sisters anymore."

"Because of a haircut?"

"I don't think Ian has any kind of job," Rochelle said. "I've never heard him talk about a job and he's always around in the daytime. He's a loser."

"He's nice," Sandra said, even though she didn't really like Ian. "He tries to be nice."

"He's nice but he's a loser. He's going to suck up all her money." The elevator doors slid open onto the carpeted lobby.

"You think he's stealing Mom's money?" Sandra asked.

"I don't think he's stealing. He's not a bad guy, he's just a useless slug. Dad's useless and he's useless. I'm not going to spend my life dragging useless people around." Rochelle was striding through the lobby, making Sandra rush to keep up. After breakfast they went to a barbershop across the street from the hotel to get Sandra's hair evened out.

"This is coming out of your paper-route money," their mother said as she pulled open the door to the barbershop.

"Just count yourself lucky that she didn't get a tattoo, that's what mine did," the barber said.

Sandra climbed into the big leather chair and closed her eyes so hair wouldn't get in them. The clippers felt nice moving over her scalp. The haircut was done in less than ten minutes.

On the way to the callback their mother bought Sandra a knitted cap with sequins sewn on it. She found the hat in a plastic basket on a table set up outside a convenience store.

"Mr. Andrews said this is the best we can do," their mother told them. Sandra bowed her head in the street. Her mother tugged the rolled-up rim down over the tips of Sandra's ears. She plucked a bright orange price tag off the front.

"And here, put these on." She took a pair of matching mittens out of the plastic bag the hat had been in.

The second casting location was an office building. Beside the elevators in the front lobby there was a burbling fountain with two fat koi fish. One, a dull white with fat whiskers, skimmed the surface as it made slow rounds of the pool. The other was smaller and brighter with glinting orange spots. Its whiskers were twitching along the aqua-coloured tiles at the bottom of the fountain. Sandra found the thick fleshiness of their whiskers unsettling.

While they were waiting for the elevator, a set of blond twins came through the revolving door into the lobby. They weren't with their mother. They had suntans. They were dressed in matching beige trench coats and boots with long thin heels.

These twins were women trapped in children's bodies or they were children convincingly disguised as women. Sandra was sure they hadn't been in the lineup in the mall basement.

Their mother asked the new twins if they were auditioning for the Tupperware commercial as well. A light had been shining out of the number 5 above the elevator doors for a long time. Sandra imagined men in jumpsuits fumbling with garbage cans on wheels and holding the doors open with outstretched arms for people with brief-cases. A small crowd packing themselves into a tight room.

"Yeah," one of them answered. She had snow in her hair, which made her suntan even more beautiful.

"Good for you."

In the elevator the new twins typed on their bejewelled phones. Their hair was styled into hard ringlets as symmetrical as the stripes on the barber's pole. One of them tilted her phone for the other to see and they laughed together.

The other twins were called in first.

"They're going to get it," Rochelle said.

"Going to this audition is a good experience," their mother said. "You'll know what to expect the next time."

Rochelle and Sandra sat on either side of their mother in a row of aluminum chairs with cushions that looked like shredded wheat. There was a round table with magazines fanned across it.

The other twins smiled at them as they left the office after their audition. The click of their skinny heels down the hall to the elevator was womanly. It was a warning that they were passing through, that they had places to click their way past at an even, determined pace.

A woman and man were inside the office. The man was sitting in an armchair and the woman stood in front of a desk with a clipboard. There were framed pictures and a big window filled with a brick wall.

"Nice to meet you both." The woman extended her hand. "Can you take off the hat, please?"

Sandra took off the hat and the woman laid her clipboard on the desk.

"I'm guessing you didn't have this hairdo at the previous audition?" She looked at the man even though she was talking to Sandra.

"No."

"Does it have to do with a health condition?" She sat on the front of the desk.

"No." Sandra's voice wobbled.

"Well, we're looking for girls with hair. Wasting people's time is not a very smart move for someone pursuing acting. I consider this a waste of my time."

"Thank you, girls, that's all," the man told them from the armchair.

Rochelle left first and Sandra pulled the door shut behind them. Their trip down the long hall to the elevator was almost soundless.

The Lodge

"YOUR MOTHER THOUGHT you might like to have these for your new place." Liam's father had arrived unannounced, holding a set of pressed curtains in a Sobeys bag.

"You're cooking," his father said. Liam realized he'd brought the spatula to the door with him.

"Just breakfast." Liam heard the shower shut off. The water stopped running and the pipes stuttered in the wall.

"There's someone here?"

"A friend. He's helping me move."

Liam's father passed him the package. There were little beads of rain on the Sobeys bag. His father edged into the apartment and Liam had to step backward to make room for him.

"New windows?" his father asked, looking into the living room.

"It's renovated." Liam skimmed a hand along the sharp

hairs growing on his jawbone. He was aware of the heat spreading across his face.

"Good, it's easier to keep a new place clean. We drove by and saw you didn't have any curtains up and your mother thought you might like to have these."

The door to the bathroom opened. The hall flooded with warm damp air and the smell of shampoo. Trent was wearing jeans and a T-shirt but his feet were bare. His hair was dripping, making dark circles on his shirt.

"This is my dad."

Trent took three steps down the hall and held out his hand. His feet left wet smudges on the floor.

"I'm Trent." Trent was taller and broader than Liam's father.

The apartment filled with a high-pitched bleating. At first it was bird-like but the louder it got the more mechanical it sounded. For a moment the three men were paralyzed by it. Trent had dropped Liam's father's hand but they were still standing close enough that they could touch. Liam held the curtains against his chest. Trent's dog barked on the back deck.

"It's a smoke alarm," Trent said. "There's something burning. Do you smell something burning?"

"It's toast," Liam said, realizing. "I was making toast under the broiler."

TRENT'S TRUCK HAD red velveteen on the ceiling. The doors and the dash were covered in panels of hard red plastic. The tape deck was broken but he had a boom box lying face up on the floor by the gearshift. It ran off a cord plugged into the cigarette lighter.

The boy standing in the drive-thru window crouched to pass them their muffins, each snug in its own little paper bag. He had tattoos down both his arms. One sleeve was outer space, with an astronaut's dome-shaped helmet gliding out from under his T-shirt, and the other was a deep-sea scene. Liam saw Trent's eyes move up and down each arm.

"Thanks, my buddy." Trent nodded at the boy and handed Liam a cardboard tray, each side sinking under the weight of a heavy paper cup.

The boy nodded. He had a streak of green running through a long side bang. The hair swished over his eye when he nodded.

Trent's truck had hips. The seats shook when it moved and there was a constant growling coming from deep inside it.

"He was cute. He was all skinny like you," Trent said, and put a hand on Liam's leg. He squeezed right above Liam's knee.

"I thought he looked like a douchebag. His hair was stupid."

They waited at the mouth of the Tim Hortons drive-way for a break in the traffic. Trent's dog was panting in the back seat, its tongue hanging slack out of the corner of its mouth.

Trent grabbed Liam's chin.

"Do you know how fucking pretty you are?" Trent asked. Liam didn't meet his eyes but Trent's hand kept his face turned toward him.

A hard lump of muscle the size of a dinner roll rose in the arm Trent was using to wrench the steering wheel. He glanced at the road and let go of Liam's face. As they pulled into the traffic, a cloud of dried leaves swirled up out of the bed of the truck.

LIAM LIFTED THREE plates and a freezer bag of cutlery out of a cardboard box on the floor. He'd cooked scrambled eggs in the cast-iron frying pan and the soggy mass seemed to be tinted a coppery green. He lifted up a little pile of egg with the spatula and tilted it from side to side in the light. He decided not to say anything.

There were no chairs. They ate standing up. Trent's hair was dripping on the linoleum. Liam held a plate on his flat palm and divided his food up with the edge of his fork.

"I was just heading out of town and I thought I'd stop in and drop off the drapes," Liam's father said again. He seemed lost, holding his fork and knife in a fist and the plate in the other hand, both in front of his chest.

"Thanks," Liam said.

"I have this beaver problem at my cabin." His father was still holding his meal out in front of him. He'd snapped his wrists lifting weights in high school and they shook. The plate wobbled in his fingers.

"They're flooding the land?" Trent laid his plate on the counter and bent over it.

"Yes. And their shit is contaminating the pond. It's very toxic."

"Beaver fever," Trent said.

"I don't know what do. They're taking over. It's a problem."

"I've taken care of beaver problems before. My buddy had a beaver infestation a few years ago. Another guy I knew had a beaver problem last summer."

"Really?" Liam's father was excited. He moved over by Trent and laid his plate on the counter too, just centimetres from Trent's. The two men's hips were practically touching, their elbows almost brushing together as they moved their utensils.

THE DOG UNDERSTOOD Trent. It could sense what he wanted. Trent just had to look at it and it hopped into the back seat or off the couch. Trent would point at the cement steps outside a convenience store or gas station and the dog would sit and wait for Trent to come out. Trent would walk out of the store without pausing or even looking at the dog and it would get up and trot behind him.

"YOU HAVE TO shoot them. It's legal if they're on your property. There's no other solution. Destroy the nest and shoot them. I've had beaver fever. Giardia, it's called. I spent a week in bed, just shaking." Trent took a big bite of toast and looked Liam's father in the face. Liam's father was nodding, the egg on his fork jiggling.

"Just shoot them?" Liam's father waved the fork in a shaky circle.

"With a registered firearm. I'm not saying I like to do it; I love animals." Trent looked over at Liam. "But there's just no other solution. Tear up the lodge and shoot them. Right in the head, be humane about it."

LIAM HAD HIS face in the pillow, a thin fold of pillow-case between his front teeth. His feet were moving without him telling them to, beating against the futon. One lifting as the other was coming down, like he was swimming.

He had glanced over his shoulder and seen Trent on his knees pouring lube into his palm.

The dog was asleep, curled up next to Liam. Its tail was resting against its front legs. Trent was holding Liam by his hipbones. His fingers were between Liam and the mattress. Liam held on to the edge of the futon frame, he gritted the pillowcase between his teeth. It didn't hurt but his eyes were watering. It wasn't pain he was feeling but something equally vivid. The bed was moving beneath him and Trent was moving on top of him and he was very still in the middle. He felt the rhythm building and he felt safe inside the steady crescendo. The dog's eyes were squinted shut, a clear drop of drool hanging from the leathery corner of its mouth.

LIAM WAS DOING Russian. His parents thought he could not have chosen a more useless degree; they were always asking if he'd think about switching to engineering like his brothers. He'd gone on a trip to Russia as part of one of his courses; it put him deeply in debt but it was worth it. He was placing some of his souvenirs around the living room when his father called.

"I'm calling about your friend."

"Trent?"

"Do you think he'd come out to the cabin and deal with the beaver problem? I'd give him a hand and I'd pay him."

Liam was setting up a line of babushka dolls on the edge of his bookcase. The dolls were painted like former leaders of Russia. Lenin was the smallest and he fit inside Stalin who fit inside Khrushchev.

"You wouldn't have to pay him, he was saying he'd like to take a run up to the cabin anyway, to check it out." Liam untwisted Yeltsin's belly and took out Gorbachev.

"I wouldn't want him doing it for free. For one thing there's the gas to get out there, and the ammo."

"He wouldn't take money. He'd be happy to do it for the family." Liam stepped back from the bookcase to see how the dolls looked from the middle of the room.

"Because he's your friend?"

"Yes."

"See, I don't want to make your mother uncomfortable. I don't have a problem with him. I just don't know how your mother will feel."

Liam inched every doll over to the left a couple of centimetres.

"He won't accept your money."

TRENT HAD A tall, narrow locker in his shed where he kept his guns. It looked just like the type of lockers that line the halls of high schools. The first time Liam went up to Trent's, Trent showed him how the locker was bolted to the wall for safety.

"So teenagers can't drive up here and break into it," Trent had said, bouncing the fat padlock on the front of the locker in his palm.

On the way out to Liam's father's cabin they pulled into East Coast Marine. Liam went with Trent to East Coast Marine regularly. Trent liked to admire guns and talk to the guys working there.

"My buddy, Reg, told me there's a really good rifle in here, half off, and if they still have it, I'm getting it," Trent told him.

The dog was riding in the back seat of the truck. Before they got out, Trent reached around and grabbed the dog by the snout. He kissed the dog between the eyes.

"You wait here, my handsome prince," Trent whispered to the dog.

Inside there was a glass display case filled with handguns; rifles were displayed in a case mounted on the wall behind the cash. Trent was asking the clerk questions. Liam dragged his hand along a rack of camo polar fleeces.

The clerk was wearing the kind of T-shirt that comes free with a case of beer, oversized and made of heavy cotton with a big logo on the chest. He held up what looked like a sugar cube box, filled with bullets. Trent picked a bullet out of the tightly packed carton and held it between his thumb and index finger. Liam saw the sharp tip dimple the pad of Trent's finger.

The clerk unlocked the case and Trent flipped open his wallet. Liam ran out to the truck and grabbed Trent's guitar case from the back seat. They zipped the gun into the case and left the store.

Trent put the case in the long silver toolbox fixed to the pan of his truck. The toolbox glittered in the sun and made Liam's eyes hurt. A man was walking through the parking lot with his daughter. She looked about thirteen. She was wearing tiny white shorts with buttons on the back pockets and she had stiff plastic hair extensions running down the length of her back. Liam could see the goosebumps on her legs. He wondered what she and her dad were doing together at East Coast Marine. Maybe getting ready to go fishing together? Or he was just picking her up from the mall and swinging by to grab some flies on the way home? They were both holding slushies in big Styrofoam cups with plastic domes on the top and they were laughing. They had stood in line together somewhere to get those drinks.

Trent stood on tiptoe and leaned across the pan to snap the latches on the toolbox shut. He and the father exchanged a manly nod while Trent was arched over the side of the truck. Liam didn't get a nod.

LIAM CALLED HIS father the morning before they left. He got out of bed and shut the door behind him. Trent was deep asleep and the alarm wouldn't go off for another fifteen minutes.

"Did you talk to Mom?"

"I talked to your mother."

"What did she say?"

"She wants the beavers gone."

"Anything else?"

"Nothing else. I told her he's a nice young man."

After he hung up Liam smoked a cigarette on the back deck. Sometimes smoking that early in the morning gave him the kind of head rush he'd gotten when he first started smoking.

THE LEAVES ON the ground were wet. They were slick, disintegrating into the mud. Both Trent and Liam's father were wearing boots. They stepped right in the little stream they were following to the beaver pool. Liam walked on the marshy edges. There was a crust of dead white moss on top of the fresh lime-green moss that was thriving beneath it. Liam's sneakers crunched through the delicate scab and filled with shockingly cold water again and again. His socks felt tight, like they were shrink-wrapping the cold against his skin.

Trent carried the gun and Liam's father carried a chainsaw. Liam was behind them with a potato picker, and a rake over one shoulder. The teeth of the rake kept catching in the brittle branches and yanking a muscle in his shoulder. The distance between him and the others was widening.

"The pool is up here, hey, Earl?" Trent called to Liam's father. The dog was bouncing through the woods just ahead of them, turning its head every few strides to make sure Trent was following. It would sometimes slow, drop its head down and sniff close to the earth, and then bound forward again.

"You're headed in the right direction," Liam's father called.

Liam could feel the armpits of his T-shirt dampening under the layers of sweaters. He hauled the neck of his shirt away from him with his free hand. His fingers were so cold they felt hot against the skin of his neck. He smelled his own sweat. And then they were at the edge of the beaver pool.

The water was flat and brown. Clumps of grey plant life floated on the surface with tendrils of translucent slime sashaying beneath them. Water doctors leapt across the surface like it was a trampoline. The little pool was surrounded by a carefully woven barrier of sticks. And, there, in the centre, a huge mound of dead branches, the bottoms sheared into spears.

Liam watched as Trent set the gun down across a boulder at the edge of the pool. He patted each side of his chest with flat palms, unbuttoned his breast pocket, and took out a granola bar. All three of them stood at the edge of the pond and listened.

WHEN THEY FINISHED, Trent lay down beside him.

"Put your head right here." He tapped a knuckle against his sternum. "Listen to my chest."

Liam put his ear over Trent's lungs. He felt the soft curls of chest hair tickle the inside of his ear. Trent breathed in deeply and his chest sank. When he exhaled Liam heard whistling inside Trent's chest. It was like wind in an old house.

"Do you hear that?" Trent moved his finger down Liam's nose, over his lips, tracing his profile.

"Yeah." Liam spoke into his chest.

"I worked under the table on a place full of asbestos when I was nineteen and no one wore a mask. It depresses the fuck out of me. I'm falling apart."

"Have you been to a doctor?" Liam asked quietly.

"It's just asthma but I'll probably die of lung cancer."

Liam reached a hand out and rubbed the top of the dog's head. It opened its mouth in a big yawn, showing two rows of yellow teeth. The dog stretched its tongue out and rolled it back in between its fangs.

"Look at my sleepy prince," Trent said.

ON THE FAR side of the water the trees gave way and there was just marsh stretching into the horizon. Trent walked along the border of woven sticks that ringed the pool and out onto the lodge. Now he was carrying the chainsaw in one hand and the gun in the other. Liam and his father stood at the edge of the pool. The dog was lying on a mossy stretch of ground, panting and squinting against the sun.

Trent walked up the mound of the nest and laid the gun down. Liam could tell from the movement of Trent's chest that he was having trouble breathing.

Liam and his father watched Trent lift the chainsaw into the air and rev the motor. He bounced the saw in the air three times, like a drummer counting into a song. And then he dug the churning chain into the nest. Bits of twig and dirt flew into the air. A damp piece of earth came down on Liam's face. He wiped at it and felt the grime spread across his cheek. Trent lifted the saw and stood still on the nest. Again they all listened.

"I don't think they're in there." Trent kicked at the sticks he'd disturbed with his steel-toed work boot.

The branches moved beneath him and both his arms shot up. A beaver swam out from under the hutch. Its bulky body glided around the bottom of the pool. The dog began to howl, a long hoarse cough with a tremble in it. Trent was swaying between the murky water and the spiked sticks with his arms in the air, trying to find his balance. His body was like a tuning fork moving with the quiver in the dog's voice.

It looked like Trent was going to stumble into the pond but he came to his knees on top of the nest. The dog jumped into the pool and stood with its legs half submerged, waiting for a command from Trent.

"Pass me the gun." Trent stood up, but he was panting and he had to lean over and rest his hands on his thighs as he tried to catch his breath.

"Jesus, are you all right?" Liam's father asked from the edge of the pool.

"Give me the gun," Trent wheezed.

"He's got asthma," Liam said.

Liam's father leaned across the pond, extending the handle of the rifle to Trent. Trent stretched his arm out and grabbed the butt of the gun. He loaded it with bullets he'd buttoned into his shirt pocket.

Trent's breathing calmed as he turned a slow circle on top of the nest, looking down into the pool. "Little fucker got away," he said, straightening up. "He's not going to come back here now because of all the racket we've been making, but there might be more in there."

The three of them spent the afternoon taking turns whacking at the nest with the chainsaw and kicking sticks into the pool. They watched the underwater entrance to the nest, waiting for another beaver to appear.

They headed back when it started getting dark. Liam's

arms were aching from lifting the chainsaw.

"Think that'll scare him away?" Liam's father asked.

"If we're lucky, that'll encourage him to move on to another stream," Trent said. "But I'd say it's likelier he'll have that all fixed by the time we get out here again."

Trent was leading them back through the woods. They had dismantled about two-thirds of the nest and left the small pond full of the debris.

Full-Body Experience

OKAY, LADIES, LET'S GO! March it, warm it up, feel that blood pumping, feel it in your muscles, we're marching, the blood is pumping, we're just getting warmed up here, ladies, are you getting warm? Okay now, sidestep!

Regina didn't know he was dead. She knew she wanted to get out of the car. The car had flipped; there was snow-caked mud and brush flattened under the passenger-side window next to her. She would have to climb into the back seat and pull herself up and out through the driver's-side window. She knew the dog was dead. When the car was spinning the dog had flown over the headrest and hit the windshield. The spinning took forever. When it stopped, the driver's-side window was full of still, grey winter sky.

Chris's head was inches from hers. He was hanging over her at an odd angle in the space between the seats; the seatbelt held his chest and hips but he was sagging

63

into the gearshift area. Regina squirmed around him, his hair brushed her neck and then her side when her T-shirt rode up. She crouched on the passenger-side door in the back seat and reached overhead to unroll the opposite window. The slow, awkward wrenching of the handle made the sheet of glass inch its way back into the door.

Let's get those knees pumping. That's it. Elbow, elbow, to the left, to the right. Lift and lift and lift. Okay now, get ready to crank it up a notch. I hope you ladies came here today to SWEAT. Let's jog. Faster, faster! We're jogging. Keep it up. This is your Serious Sweat class, it's what you make of it. Faster, faster.

The dog rolled off the dash; it had blood in its nostrils. Regina could see it wasn't breathing because the blood didn't ripple or bubble. This was after the car had stopped moving, after she had wriggled against the smothering, warm weight of her boyfriend to get into the back seat. She didn't listen to his chest. Or do CPR. She didn't look at his face.

You're really letting me down, ladies! Next time I say high kick I want to see some high kicks. Okay, here it comes: high kick! Oh yeah, there you go, left hook, right hook, high kick, that's what I was waiting for, that's what I call a high kick, okay here we go again, give it to me again, ladies, one hundred and ten percent, one hundred and ten percent of the time, right hook, left hook — last time — high kick, tricked you last time for real, let's see it — high kick. When I say high kick, I mean HIGH KICK.

She stood up on the door of the overturned car in the January air, panting. She had put her hands on either side of the window and lifted her body up out of the car, the way you haul yourself out of the deep end onto the pool deck. There was a stretch of dead bushes sticking out of the snow and a steep slide of ditch between her and the highway. She'd taken her sneakers off before the accident. They had been listening to the Quebec election results, heat pouring out of the dash. She had crossed her legs on the seat and unzipped her hoodie and said something like "Do you think Brittany was annoyed when Carl said she misunderstood the end of *Inception*?" or "Do you think that storm is really going to come? I hope the supermarkets don't close, there's nothing to eat at the house."

Let's cool it down, let's get ready to stretch it out. Okay, inhale as you enter the twist, exhale as you release. A little deeper. And again. See if you can go a little deeper this time.

AFTER THE FUNERAL Regina went lane swimming all the time; underwater was a private realm. She was constantly afraid that she'd left the burner on or the bathtub running or the front door unlocked. Every night she'd lie in bed trying to visualize herself turning the knobs on the stove, and she wouldn't be able to, so she would run down the stairs in a floppy T-shirt and double-check.

ELINOR WAS COMPACT: teeny-tiny, but lumpy with muscles. She was from Nova Scotia. Her hair was dyed white and she wore it in a high ponytail with a little bump in the front where her bangs were pinned up. The gym director introduced them in the lobby.

"Elinor is our new Buff Bar instructor," he told Regina. Then his hand flew up and touched a red light flashing on his headset. "That's my wife," he said to them. "I'll let you finish up the introductions — yes, hi, I'm here." He walked away from the two women, pressing the earpiece into his head with two fingers.

"I'm Regina, I do Pilates and Serious Sweat."

"That's great, I'm hoping they'll let me have a few more classes once I've been here for a while. I taught a lot of dance classes at the Y in Halifax; they said they're not interested in that in my interview but maybe I can change their minds." Elinor was drinking a smoothie out of a reusable cup. "I'd love to get a drink sometime, I just moved here."

Her ponytail swished back and forth as she walked down the hall toward the change rooms.

Regina sat in the parking lot and called Viv; Viv had become the person she told about her day. Viv was who she texted to say that she was hungry but didn't know what to eat.

"Viv, they hired someone new at the gym and she sucks."

"Oh no, why does she suck?" Viv was dependable like that.

"She's so primped. She's the kind of person who thinks

an exercise class should look like a music video. I can't stand that."

"Regina, you should try to make friends, fill your life with people. Don't shut them out," Viv said.

Regina and Viv had met at a party a few years ago. Emilio, another instructor at Regina's gym had introduced them.

If Regina could have anyone else's body it would be Emilio's. She often watched him practising dance routines in unbooked studios at the gym. Sometimes the elasticity of his body was disturbing; it seemed like there was nothing beneath his skin but muscle. As though he didn't have bones to keep him from transforming into a slippery puddle if he willed it.

At parties they'd hang around the smokers. She and Emilio with their cuffs pulled over their knuckles and collars zipped up to their chins on the back deck, waiting to be offered cigarettes.

Emilio had a French accent and striking cheekbones. He flirted with everyone, lied easily, was a master shoplifter. The night she met Viv was a New Year's Eve party, before she and Chris got together, and she'd been in a bathroom with Emilio and Timothy Argueta, a dancer who'd come from Vancouver to visit Emilio. The three of them were smoking two cigarettes, passing them back and forth, watching their reflections in the mirror. She and Emilio had kissed. Then she and Tony Argueta kissed. Then she sank into a wide squat and nuzzled their hard cocks through their jeans with her face while they made out with each other. Even though they were both very uninterested in her, it was the sexiest thing that had ever happened to her. Emilio didn't come to the funeral, but he left a voicemail saying how sorry he was.

And before the accident she used to go jogging almost every day with Lucy, who taught Owning Toning and Advanced Cyclelates. She texted Regina after the accident and invited her out for coffee and over for dinner, but Regina never responded. She couldn't imagine talking to Lucy without the rhythm of their sneakers beating gravel.

Now Regina pretty much only hung out with Viv. Viv drove her home from the hospital after the accident. The doctors had put on a fibreglass cast that turned her hand into an unusable claw. Viv made her a pasta salad from what was in the fridge. She opened the child-proofed plastic lid of Regina's painkillers for her because Regina couldn't grip the bottle and the lid at the same time.

Viv came by every day the week after that. She bought Regina a new cover for her futon. It was light pink with ripples of purple tie-dye and Regina hated it. She sat in the armchair as Viv zipped her couch into the new cover.

"You don't need to spend money on me. I appreciate you coming over but don't waste your money," Regina told her.

"You need to change things up," Viv said.

The painkillers hurt Regina's stomach and made her exhausted.

Viv arrived with a new shower curtain, see-through with multi-coloured polka dots.

"Let's have a dinner party here, I'll cook." Viv was putting a pizza box Regina had left in the living room into a see-through recycling bag.

"Maybe when the cast comes off," Regina told her.

The week the cast came off she got dressed up because Viv said she should. Viv had just gotten a job at a spa that had opened downtown and she wanted Regina at the launch party. She didn't say "if you're ready."

Regina laid her crushed-velvet mini dress on the bed and thought about whether to wear her hair up or down. The skin on her hand felt raw after having been wrapped in gauze for five and a half weeks. Looking in the mirror she was surprised by how proud she felt of the way her clothes hung on her body.

At the party, people kept coming up to her asking her how she knew Viv and if she'd gone to massage therapy school. She was thinking about her stove. She made herself rum and Cokes at a little table covered with twenty-sixers and two-litre bottles of pop. People were dancing and the lights were low. A man was tossing his head back and forth while unbuttoning his shirt.

"This is my friend Regina, she teaches aerobics," Viv said again and again.

Regina shook their hands but she was thinking about a red coil burning in a dark kitchen.

She would find herself shivering and distracted in the supermarket. She would stare at the beans so that no one could tell she was being swept away.

THE PLACE SHE got swept to was vast. It could fit a lot of "we weren't really in love anymore" and "I never got to tell him what a piece of shit he was for pressuring me into anal sex" and "I will never meet another man romantic enough to haul the car off the road every time he saw a glimmering hunk of calcium in a cliff and chip me down a crystal with the screwdriver and mallet he kept in the trunk." Also "a man who insisted on meeting my grandmother" and "I don't remember locking the front door" and "I don't remember unplugging the kettle" and "how do you know if the batteries in the smoke detector are worn out?" Big enough to get very lost in.

She brought a cat home from Heavenly Creatures and filled the apartment with plants. Viv noted this and took it as a sign that Regina was recovering, that she was embracing life in its various forms again. Partly she was and partly she was building a sarcophagus. Regina picked ropey plants, plants with vines and tendrils, the better to wrap around her limbs and cocoon her body. The better to worm themselves through her nostrils and between her lips and into her ear canals, the better to unfurl their leaves in her anal cavity. She pictured the cat lovingly chewing through her fingers.

At first the cat ran from noise; it sprayed the couch and her shoes and coats. She read about training cats. If a cat pees on your bed, it's because he trusts you, he's seeking out the smell of you. The second time it happened she didn't have the energy to strip the bed and wait for the sheets to go through the washer and dryer. It was freezing and she was alone and the pee was down in the bottom corner. So she slept there with their smells mingling and making a new smell. His pee mixing with the smell of her armpits.

"THIS REMINDS ME of when I lived in Halifax with Brian, my ex-boyfriend." Regina had invited Elinor over for a drink so she could tell Viv about it later and seem like she was making an effort to be social. "There was a heat wave and the garbage collectors were on strike," Elinor was saying. "The whole city stank. We'd just moved there and neither of us had jobs yet — we hardly had any furniture but we had a futon and a blender and we used to make margaritas and sit naked under the ceiling fan in the living room." Elinor was twirling her empty wine glass by the stem.

"How does this remind you of that?" Regina lifted the wine bottle at Elinor, who put her glass down on the table to be filled.

"Being drunk in the heat. A new city. Getting to know someone."

"You didn't know him?" Regina finished pouring Elinor's wine and filled her own glass.

"I knew him better than I know you but I didn't know him inside out. I was still surprised he moved there for me. The room didn't have an overhead light and we didn't have any lamps and we would just sit there while it got dark. In the summer it takes a long time to get dark. In winter it happens without you noticing but in summer it takes forever."

Regina had a pinky's width of wine left in the glass she had just poured.

"We could get naked now, it's hot enough," Regina said. She tipped the last sip into her mouth and stuck her tongue out after swallowing. The music had stopped so she got up to put on a new song.

"How drunk are you?" Elinor asked.

"I'm a lightweight." Regina leaned into the iPod, squinted and brought her face close to it.

"Good, because I'm really drunk."

Regina couldn't pick a song because every song was from before the accident. The wine had sucked all the moisture out of her mouth.

"Let's put on your iPod," Regina said.

"Are we going to get naked?" Elinor asked. "I was kind of into getting naked."

"Put on your iPod and then we'll get naked."

Elinor took her phone out of her purse. She jostled the speaker cord into the phone and there was a burst of static that sounded like a wave crashing, but then the cord clicked in and a pop song came blaring out of the speaker louder than either of them had expected. They opened another bottle of wine and left their jeans on the kitchen floor.

"You don't shave," Elinor said.

"Does that gross you out?"

"It's just weird to me, I've always done it, since I was like twelve. I can't imagine."

Elinor banged her head against a potted plant that hung from the ceiling of the bedroom. Some soil fell on the carpet and the plant swung like a pendulum for a moment, the leaves waving on their stalks. Elinor pressed a palm into her forehead and they both laughed.

Regina could tell that Elinor had been wearing a tube-top bikini when she got her fake tan. Her breasts and a narrow strip on her back were bright white. The bottoms had left her ass and crotch and hips almost glowing against the orange sheen on the rest of her skin. They danced and drank out of the bottle. Regina knocked the lip of the bottle against her front teeth. Elinor jumped and hit the ceiling with her palm.

Regina fell back onto the futon and splashed the new cover with wine. Elinor shuffled toward her until Regina's lips were pressed against a muscle that bulged on Elinor's hipbone. Elinor put her fingernails in Regina's hair, dragged it up into a ponytail, and gave it a tug. Then she and Elinor were making out in bed, Elinor's crotch was wet against her thigh. A draft of wind was trapped in the closet; she could hear the empty coat hangers knocking elbows. Elinor's strange white hair swished across the pillows and for a second it looked like the foamy aftermath of a winter wave sliding over wet sand.

When she woke up it felt like her mouth was full of napkins. Elinor was curled into herself, her spine facing Regina. The cat was a sloppy Kaiser bun on Elinor's pillow. Regina's pulse was loud inside her head and the smell of alcohol was leaking out of her skin. She had let the whole night happen without mentioning Chris. She threw up in the toilet and showered while Elinor slept.

She had jumped off the car into the snow and pain had vibrated in her knees and heels with the force of hitting the ground. She'd got tangled in the brush. She had to lift her knees high over and over again to make it to the ditch. The crust of ice on top of the snow was sharp and it hurt her through her jeans. She couldn't go back for her sneakers because she was afraid a car would pass and she would miss the chance to flag it down.

Regina put on her winter coat and went out on the back deck to call Viv. Her hair was wet from the shower and when the cold air hit, it froze a little. There was no answer so she left a message.

"So, there are things that me and Elinor have in common," she said. "We're both fucked over by the gym in the same way, no job stability, no long-term contracts. She understands the pressure to keep people coming back, like how you have to make a class hard but not too hard, you have to charm them and scare them at the same time. Okay, I'll call you later." She had prepared this speech in the shower before making the call. The cat was watching her through the kitchen window.

Regina heard Elinor waking up and she put coffee on. Elinor came out of the bedroom carrying a pair of boxer shorts.

"Who do these belong to?"

Regina flicked open the stovetop espresso maker. The heat stung her eyes, that dizzy moment on top of the car, feeling the cold metal through her socks, the smell of burnt rubber in the freezing air.

Elinor was swinging the underwear on one finger, teasing. She flicked it across the room. Regina let the lid fall shut.

Elinor started at the snap of metal on metal. "I don't care. I'm just surprised you didn't mention. There are worse things — you could be a blabbermouth."

Elinor normally wore her silver hair straightened but it had plumped overnight.

"I made coffee," Regina said.

After Elinor left, Regina folded up the underwear and dropped it in the garbage. She tugged a microwave-popcorn bag out from under some coffee grounds and covered the boxers with it. She fed the cat.

They'd never lived together, but still his things kept turning up, as if they were bubbling up from the depths of the house. A coat that belonged to Chris was hung inside her winter parka. An energy drink in the very back of the fridge, something she never would have bought. The coat, she remembered the day he left the coat, it was the beginning of winter and he'd worn it over to her place and left it because suddenly it smelled like spring. The seasons had been stuttering, trying to sprawl into winter but jolting back to fall again and again.

ELINOR HAD HER foot up on the bench tying her sneakers when Regina came into the change room after Serious Sweat.

"Come to my house for dinner tonight. I'm going to roast a chicken and we can have some wine," Elinor said.

"I have to feed the cat."

"Come over after you feed the cat."

Elinor hadn't finished moving into her apartment. One cupboard was completely empty except for three water glasses crowded together and pushed up against the wall.

"I'm so lonely it's getting to the point where I dread interacting with people. I try on every piece of clothing I own before I go out," Regina was saying as she stirred the gravy.

Elinor was wearing a pair of pleather leggings and a baggy T-shirt. Her hair was in a bun on top of her head.

They got drunk again. On the way to the bathroom Regina passed Elinor's bedroom. The only furniture was the bed. Four duffle bags were slung around the room with tangles of clothes slouching out of them. Elinor's exercise sneakers were carefully lined up at the end of the bed and her headset was resting on top of them.

"Your house is so empty. You should get some stuff for the walls." Regina settled back into her seat.

"Lucy told me about your boyfriend," Elinor said. "I mean she only told me yesterday. I didn't know that night we had drinks."

There was a little dent in Regina's chest where one of her ribs had crumpled in on itself. She'd snapped a bone in her hand trying to brace herself against the dash.

It had been bright in the operating room and "New York Groove" was playing on the radio. The drugs didn't knock her out, but she couldn't lift her head and tears streamed out of the corners of her eyes. The outside fold of her ear filled with tears and overflowed.

She was only now beginning to be able to do a full push-up on that hand.

"We weren't even happy." Regina stroked the dent in her side without realizing she was doing it.

"You have to move out of that apartment," Elinor said. "Just move out. You'll feel better."

WHEN HER THINGS were gone, Regina went for the final walk-through. Like reading over an exam to make sure you haven't made any slip-ups. It could have been anyone's apartment. The cat had scratched up part of the patio rail. The windows were open and the noise of leaves shivering against each other had the hint of a wave sucking out into the bay, but there was also the smell of hot pavement.

Boxes were stacked in the hallway and kitchen of her new place. Regina hadn't brought the plants. She'd dropped them out her old bedroom window one by one and watched the pots smash in a dumpster that was pushed up against her building. Viv had helped her carry the futon up the stairs. Her dishes and pans were still packed up but she bought groceries and made a cheese melt by laying the bread right on the oven rack.

Regina unrolled her mat on the floor of her new living room. She dragged a lamp into the room and looked around for an outlet. She slapped a notepad on the floor and put her headphones in and started drafting a new class.

Most of the people in Regina's classes were women between forty and sixty. They came for Pilates on their lunch break or aerobics when they finished work for the day. They worked for the government or the university or they were retired teachers. They were there because they wanted to ease the transition into old age, they wanted to protect their knees and hips by encasing them in muscle, they wanted to stay mobile, they wanted to counteract years of sitting.

This class is about flow, Regina wrote. *Every transition is going to be graceful. Okay, palms on your mat, bend your knees. Everyone should be on all fours. Slide your left arm under you, put your shoulder and cheek on the mat. Flip onto your back; gentle, smooth transitions, ladies. Sink your shoulders into the floor, stretch your arms above your head, point your toes.*

There were injuries she didn't learn she'd sustained until later. No one can predict the long-term effects, the doctor had told her. Embedded in her forearm were five chunks of windshield glass that would never come out. A string of raised lumps going up her arm, an island chain caught between muscle and skin.

Serving

Dave

They give you four litres to drink and they say to chill it to make it go down easier. It's like milk. The way milk sticks to the inside of your mouth. It just coats your tongue. You unscrew the top and it glug-glugs out like windshield wash. It doesn't go down your throat easy and it sits in your belly like a four-pound ice cube.

There was an MRI and I don't do well with enclosed spaces, ever since I was a child. My older brother locked me in a trunk when we were playing hide and seek on Easter Sunday. I could hear all the adults gathering around the trunk. I could see through the slats—tan pants and black tights. They were saying, "Jesus Christ, how are we going to get him out of there?"

The whole time I was in the trunk I was hyperventilating, with my knees tucked into my chest. My aunt was screaming about the trunk getting beat up. I started trying to slow my breathing down, trying to inch my knees out of my throat, trying to make enough room that I didn't suffocate myself. In the end they had to take the latch off the front with a crowbar to get me out.

And when they open you up from that end for a colonoscopy, the air rushes in and then it's got to come back out. The pain and the stink. Some people are fine an hour later; I spent an entire day locked in the bathroom, sweating.

I didn't tell anyone that the doctor said I had to go in for tests, not even Sharon. I made the appointment for a Wednesday morning because Sharon's always working then. She'd be all antsy waiting for the results and I'd rather not think about it until I'm actually hearing it from the doctor.

But Marlene just knew. We were splitting a table of fifteen. The two of us hip to hip by the garbage, scraping plates at an ungodly pace. Marlene reaches behind me to grab a dish pan; I drop a scraped plate into it. We anticipate the twist and turn of each other's bodies like a figure skating team.

"Dave, you look grey," Marlene says.

"Yeah, Marlene, I know I'm grey."

"Your face is grey. You're not well."

"No, Marlene, I'm not well. This place has crawled up my hole and it's poisoning me from the inside out."

"I'll get the bills and the chocolates, you get the hot towels."

Patrick

I'm waiting for my father to finish work. Mom used to pick him up but last month she was watching *Lethal Weapon 2* on TV and it was almost over when Dad called to be picked up so she asked me to go. Now I do it three or four times a week.

He storms out of the restaurant, leather shoes and dress pants, swishing down the steps and over to the car. His shoes have wrinkles in them, a huge crease near the laces with thinner wrinkles growing out of it.

"Every single one of them is a fucking imbecile. I'm not doing it anymore. I'm not. They can find someone else because I'm done." He reels out a variation of that speech almost every time I pick him up.

Next he stares out the windshield and puts his hands on his head. He moves his fingers up over his forehead into his hairline and says, "Just give me a minute."

When his hair went grey it went slack. He likes pointing his hair out in old photos. When he was younger it was dirty blond and up until I was about eleven he wore it in a curly halo. Since he started balding he keeps it short.

On nights that I pick him up we sit in the car with the smell of cooked food hanging on him. For maybe fifteen minutes he'll massage his scalp while looking at the bumper of the car parked in front of us.

He'll undo a button and reach inside his shirt to unclip his name tag. There's a magnetic strip that goes inside the shirt and holds the plate with his name etched on it in place. After he puts the name tag in his breast pocket

I turn the key and we pull away from the front of the restaurant.

"You don't smoke do you, Pat? Never start smoking, I'll never stop missing it," he'll say. I'm always grateful that Duckworth Street is quiet on weeknights. I've had my licence for almost a year but I still get nervous looking over my shoulder to switch lanes. Dad barks at me if I go slow or hesitate before changing lanes.

Some nights Marlene gets a ride home with us. Those nights are easier. We stop at the McDonald's or Tim Hortons drive-thru. I drive and Dad nods along with Marlene while she complains about their shift from the back seat.

"I don't care who you are, what kind of a restaurant it is, you don't show up to waitress in those kind of boots." This is the type of thing Marlene is usually saying as we crawl through a drive-thru. Dad agrees with those types of sentiments. Marlene likes to uncrank the back window a little and light a cigarette.

When Mom and Dad smoked they never smoked in the car. It depreciates the value of the car; the smell gets into the upholstery. My friend Kevin bought his older brother's car and no one's allowed to smoke in it because it depreciates the value.

"And just in general," Marlene is adding, "regardless of your employment, you shouldn't bleach the shit out of your hair like that. I mean, she's ruined it. It'll take years to grow that out."

"Unless she cut it off short?" my dad asks. "Jesus, Patrick, he's letting you go, get in the fucking lane."

"She couldn't, she doesn't have the jawline for it, you have to have a jawline for that kind of a haircut, Dave."

"What do you guys want?" I ask as we pull up to the speaker where they take your order.

"That's something we don't hear every day, now isn't it, Marlene? What do we want?" My dad is cracking up at his own joke while the girl on the other side of the drive-thru speaker waits for our order.

Dave

Be approachable but don't fawn. Create an atmosphere where they're your superiors. "Can I take that out of your way?" Make them feel it. "Sorry to reach across."

Some people crave that. They enjoy the theatre of it and take pride in knowing their lines.

"We'll have a bottle of that Merlot; let my wife taste it, though, she's got the palate between us."

Other people get uncomfortable. They keep trying to let you know that they're just like you. "I waitressed all through college." But that works too. Guilt is a powerful incentive to tip. Go with it.

It gets to be that you know every part of it. When you close your eyes at night you see the carpet. Navy blue with a pattern of burgundy diamonds, staple-gunned to the inside of your eyelids. You know the choreography of sliding a large tin of tomatoes in front of the door to the laundry room with your shoe when your arms are

full of tablecloths. You know you can lay the lid of the
hot-towel steamer on the little ledge above it if you need
to get towels and only have one free hand. Your knees
and ankles and wrists and lower back ache all day every
day from carrying heavy dishes. Lifting plates up and
down from the table to the tray and back again, all that
standing. Each pang of pain—your wrist when you flick
the paper open in the morning, your knee when you take
the garbage out, your lower back as you bend down to
undo your shoes—means the routine has crept right into
your joints. There's a smell on your hands and in your hair
at the end of the night. It thins your hair out. Your body
ends up like a mop that's been dragged across the floor
too many times, all the stringy extremities bloated with
the grime of the place.

Marlene gets me because she's very intuitive. But it's
not just that, we're on the same wavelength. Marlene can't
stand the idea of having some twenty-year-old telling her
how to do her job, and I wouldn't know the first thing
about putting a resumé together. We're in the same boat,
too old to start somewhere new.

Patrick
Me and Kathy always hang out at her house. Her parents are renovating, they're turning the basement into an
apartment they can rent out. There's a stove and a fridge
and a living room with a couch. There's a small room
with a single bed in it. We aren't allowed to close the door

to that room but we do. Her parents come home around twenty to six. They bring us sub sandwiches, twisted in wax paper and knotted in individual tube-shaped plastic bags. Or they make spicy pasta with sausage in it. Or Shake 'n Bake chicken legs. Sometimes they order pizza.

In the room her electric guitar is propped on a stand in the corner and there's a dartboard. There's a small rectangular window high up in the wall. It's half filled with grass and half filled with sky. We lie on the narrow bed with our sneakers on, ready to hop up and open the door if we hear feet on the stairs. I rub inside her jeans, over her underwear, sometimes for an hour. She puts her mouth around my cock over my underwear and breathes, making the material damp with her breath. We shimmy our pants down to mid-thigh and rub against each other. We are very careful not to make the bed whine. We know which rooms her parents are in by tracking their footsteps above us. My boxers get ground into my balls. I can almost feel how everything would fit without the fabric. If it was a real apartment, we would just glide together.

Dave

There are bands that I love. I hardly drink but I like a toke as much as the next guy. I love Deep Purple. I love sitting in my chair listening to Deep Purple. Smoke a joint and listen to Deep Purple, that's a Sunday afternoon for me.

I never thought they would come here. Then a couple of the roadies are in the restaurant and Marlene's serving them and telling them about how I love Deep Purple and she calls me over. They say to come down with an ID, we'll put your name on the door, bring a friend.

I'm thinking I'll take Sharon, we don't get out to things very often. Sharon is getting to the point where coming to pick me up at eleven or twelve is too late for her. So she sends Patrick down for me most nights. I don't mind that, some days she's up at five thirty to be into Pipers for six, but I do miss driving home at the end of the night with her. Now she's usually out cold in the bed with the TV going when we get in. Shutting the TV off wakes her up and then I tell her a little bit about my night.

"Take Patrick, he'd love that," she says, half asleep. "Something with his dad. I don't want to be out half the night at a loud concert."

"You think Patrick would like that?"

"There you go," Sharon says into her pillow. I wrap myself around her so my cheek is up against her shoulder blade. I hate getting in bed with the smell of the restaurant on me — some nights I get a shower — but tonight I'm too tired.

WE HAVE TO park all the way up by the restaurant because downtown is just blocked. Mile One isn't anywhere near full, though, and the audience is all men. The place is packed with grey heads. Guys like me. Some fat fuck down in the front with his shirt off, waving it around. There are five or six girls in the row below us, but they're all sitting on their hands, looking around at these old grey assholes, that idiot in the front waving his T-shirt. They're disappointed too. Patrick has this slack face on him. I keep telling him to go down and say hi to the girls before the show starts.

"Get one of them to come sit in that seat next to you, I don't mind," I say to him. The girls stand up and call out to some guys coming down the aisle with beer. I wave to the girls and point at Patrick, just ribbing him for fun, and he won't even crack a smile.

Then the band comes out. I'm like who the fuck is this? I only recognize the drummer and the guy on bass. Instead of two guitars they've got one young guy. He looks like maybe twenty and he's just wanking off his own interpretation. And the singer, I don't know who the fuck they have, he's wearing this big boot like he has a broken foot. Wandering around the stage clunking the broken foot. Couldn't hit a high note if his life depended on it. I'm like just stand still and sing the fucking song. I can't even recognize the songs. I'm listening to the words trying to figure out what song it is: couldn't tell you. Then they do the chorus of "Smoke on the Water" and the place goes up. I say to Patrick, "Let's get out of here." We just leave. I'm not cheering for a fouled-up version of the song.

It's early enough that Marlene will be getting off. "We'll just stop in to the restaurant and see if Marlene needs a ride," I tell Patrick, since we're heading that way to get the car. It's a warm night; we both take off our fall jackets as we walk. "You don't mind that we left the concert, do you?"

"I don't care."

"You're still crooked at me for waving at those girls? Loosen up, can't you have a little fun with your dad?" He looks away from me and I think it's because I made him smile a bit in spite of himself.

Marlene is just leaving the restaurant as we're coming up Queen's Road.

"I thought the two of you were out for a night on the town!" she calls out to us.

"Marlene, you wouldn't believe that concert. We had to leave, didn't we, Patrick? Tell her what a disaster it was."

"It wasn't great." Patrick is playing along.

"What a night we had at the restaurant, Dave," Marlene says. "I had a table of fifteen to myself and then it was tables of three and four all night. I made more money than I've made all month." Marlene is flushed.

"I shouldn't have wasted my time at that friggin' concert. I gave Paul my shift, I suppose he made a shitload in tips?" I ask her.

"Let me buy you a beer," Marlene says. "You're not underage, are you, Patrick?"

"I'm seventeen."

"Well, don't you worry, they'll give you a beer out of pity when they see who you're hanging out with." Marlene puts an arm around Patrick's shoulders.

We end up at O'Mally's, where two young guys are onstage doing a Great Big Sea cover. We get a table for three and a pint for each of us. I barely drink anymore, I'll have one or two beers, that's it. Even that makes me a bit silly. So the pint loosens me right up.

"How's your health, Dave?" Marlene asks me when Patrick is in the bathroom.

"The colonoscopy showed it could be prostate cancer."

"Jesus, what are they saying? Do you need chemo or radiation or what?"

"They don't know anything yet. The tumour could be benign."

"Sharon must be losing it with worry," Marlene says.

"I haven't told Sharon." As I say it I notice Patrick is out of the bathroom and not far from the table; I'm hoping the music has drowned us out. "Anyway, it might be nothing, so."

"Jesus Christ, a colonoscopy is *something*. You have to tell her—even if it's benign, it's something." Patrick is definitely within earshot now but Marlene's got her back to him.

"Marlene," I say, trying to shut her up.

Patrick is at the table.

"Some band, hey?" Marlene's got this stupid smile on her face.

Patrick

My mother works at Pipers. She has two orange aprons that fasten on the sides with Velcro. Sometimes she has to wear pins that advertise a sale. She keeps them in a little stack next to her name tag on the laundry shelf. She plays cards one night a week with the women she works with, sometimes at our place and sometimes at theirs. They do Secret Santa every year at Christmas and they send each other emails with dirty jokes. There are a few that she calls on the phone just to talk.

Mom and I are usually home alone together on the weeknights. Dad goes to work at four in the afternoon and most days I don't get back from Kathy's until after he's gone. Some nights I eat two suppers, once at Kathy's and again at home. Mom and I sit in the kitchen and watch the tiny TV on the counter while we eat.

"Your father didn't enjoy the concert, I heard," my mother says, lowering the volume on the television with the remote.

"I didn't want to go anyway—Deep Purple is dad rock." She's just taken up a forkful of food but she starts laughing and has to lay it back down on the plate.

"And he was embarrassing me. He kept waving at these girls, like for a joke, and pointing at me. He totally creeped them out."

"Your father lacks some social graces."

"That's an understatement."

Mom loses it again, she starts coughing with food in her mouth.

"Is Dad sick?" I ask her.

"What? Sick?"

"At the bar he was saying something to Marlene about getting a colonoscopy, I think."

"About him getting a colonoscopy? He was saying this to Marlene?"

"I think so, I don't know. Don't say I said. I just over-heard them talking about it. Marlene was talking about a colonoscopy and a benign tumour."

"What exactly was he saying?" Mom stands up and takes our plates off the table.

"I don't know."

There's still a big clump of potato on my plate; when she lays hers on top of it the potato squishes out between the rims and gets on her hand. She drops the plates in the sink and holds her hand up, showing the white smear on her palm. She looks around for something to wipe it on.

"Your father shouldn't have taken you to a bar in the first place."

"We weren't there for very long." I stand up and start unloading the dishwasher to make room for the plates.

"I can't take this tonight. It's too much after I've worked all day." Mom starts scraping cooked-on scalloped pota-toes out of the bottom of a roasting pot with a wooden spoon. The pot has been soaking in the sink since Mom took up dinner. Sudsy bubbles rise up out of the white mush. She has a plate done up for Dad, sitting in the microwave, covered in plastic wrap.

"The keys are on the coffee table. Can you pick him up again?"

"Sure." I click the dishwasher shut, still half full of clean dishes.

"It's not too much to ask? Do you have a test or anything tomorrow?" My mother is reaching for the cordless landline with a hand that glistens with dish soap. A slick whirl of iridescent blue and purple with streaks of burgundy, lit up by the light on the stove.

"I can do it," I tell her.

I hear the seven beeps of a phone number being dialled as I walk down the hall.

"Helen, I just sent Patrick to pick Dave up again," I hear her saying. She's lowered her voice a little but I can still hear her as I lace up my sneakers. "I just can't look at him right now."

I want to keep listening but if my mother doesn't hear the front door open she'll know I'm eavesdropping. I'm wishing I hadn't said anything.

Dave

TIPS IN FEBRUARY

- Gas
- Chicken, ground beef, liver, sandwich meat, bread, milk, a package of Fudgeos
- Rum for Sharon's card night
- New socks and underwear for myself
- Half the heat bill

Sharon is a saint. I don't mean she puts up with bullshit. She's not like that. And if you want to talk about the bedroom, she knows what she's doing. I got no complaints that way. Zero complaints in that department.

Me and Marlene isn't that kind of a thing. I'll be happy with Sharon for the rest of my natural-born life. I don't think I'm the best thing since sliced ham either, just to be clear. I know about my many flaws; I know I have flaws I don't even know about.

Partly I just haven't worked out a good time to tell her and if it's nothing there's no need to tell. I'm not religious but I'm a bit superstitious. I don't believe positive thinking cures cancer or anything like that. Just there's a part of me that thinks saying it out loud is bad luck.

Patrick

Kathy's parents are at a funeral. Before they left, her mother stood in front of the open fridge in the outfit she'd picked out. She was wearing a tight, knee-length skirt and a blazer. She had her hair twisted into a knot on the back of her head. The hairs growing on her neck were tugged tight by the bun, lifting little buds of flesh at the base of each hair. My mother doesn't dress up in that way, to be sexy. For a funeral she wears slacks and a cardigan with two rows of gold buttons on the front.

"There's lots of food here. You can make sandwiches for lunch. There's mayonnaise and ham there. I just bought a fresh loaf of bread yesterday," Kathy's mother said. She had a black leather purse with a long, thin strap hung over her shoulder.

"I'm sorry for your loss," I said.

"That's sweet of you, Pat," Kathy's mother said into the fridge.

We listened to the car pull out of the driveway and to be safe we made sandwiches and left them sitting out on the counter. We left the mayonnaise open with a butter knife sticking up out of the thick sauce and the bread slouching out of the mouth of the open bag.

Kathy's bedroom is filled with middle-of-the-day light. She has a spongy foam pad under her sheet and four pillows. We're under her duvet with our jeans and socks on. Kathy lies on top of me. She smells like her house. I slide my hand between her jeans and her underwear and squeeze her butt. It's hot under the duvet and Kathy pulls her sweater off. As the sweatshirt comes over her head a tug of static electricity sweeps her eyebrows upward. She settles back onto the mattress beside me and I undo her jeans.

My elbows are sinking into the mattress on either side of her hips. I don't have a clear sense of exactly what I'm supposed to do. Her knees are towering over me. I try to move my tongue like I would my hand.

"Slower."

"What?" I lift my head but I can't look her in the eyes.

"Can you do it slower?"

She starts breathing short, quick breaths out of her nose. My hard-on is pressing into the bed. I undo my pants and kick them down into the blankets and then lean into her again.

"Katherine?" We hear Kathy's mother call out and a

half a second later we hear the front door shut. Heels on the hardwood floor.

Kathy wiggles up the bed and sits up straight; she still has her T-shirt on. I reach back and forth under the blankets for my pants.

"Yeah?" Kathy is fumbling her way into her underwear.

Kathy's mother pushes the door open. She sees us and spins around. She stands in the doorway with her back to us for a moment before walking away.

"Katherine, I want to talk to you," she says from the end of the hall.

"Okay." Kathy jumps out of bed and pulls her jeans on, they're tight and she has to bend her knees and move her hips and suck her tummy in to get them on.

I can't get the button on my pants done up because my hands are shaking. There's a mirror on the wall in the hallway and I can see their reflection, standing close together.

"He's not allowed over here anymore," Kathy's mother is saying.

Dave

See, the thing with me and Marlene. With me and Marlene, when the dining room is full, we just forget about the sections chart. We just run appetizers and set tables and take drink orders and split the tips down the middle at the end of the night. And whatever new airhead they've got blathering on to Dennis at the front end, saying "How do you make a margarita?" or "Do I bring the towels now or after the bill?" — we just ignore them, let them drown out there. If they're any good they'll get the hang of it, and if not they'll have a good cry and quit.

Marlene zips around flicking new tablecloths out and I follow her with cutlery and side plates. We don't have to say a word to each other. We get into a rhythm. Whole nights just blur by, all the little routines click together like Lego and then the evening is done.

When I have to work with those other eejits all I think about is how much easier the night would be with Marlene. The worst of it is they talk and talk and talk. Non-stop blathering. If I've got five seconds I like to just watch my tables and enjoy a bit of silence. Marlene understands that.

And there's me and Marlene sharing a draw out back at the end of the shift. It's not something we do every night. Just on those nights when we're sharing a bunch of big tables. She's got this little case, just big enough for a lipstick, you flip the lid and there's a rectangular mirror in there. She keeps it behind the bar and checks her lipstick all night long. Takes her all of three seconds to fix her lipstick. The case has a magnetic flap and it snaps shut.

Patrick
My parents have a telephone set up on a little side table by their bed. It has a thick curly cord connecting the receiver to the body of the phone and it's tethered to the wall by a

thin grey cord. Tonight I'm walking by my parents' bed-room when the phone rings, but my mother gets to it in the kitchen at the same time I do. I rest the mouthpiece against my neck just below my ear to listen.

"Hello?" a woman says.

"Margie? Hi, what's all the news?" It's my mother's friend.

I get down on the floor and lift the bed skirt. Under their bed is a cool, dark expanse. My parents are very clean.

"Oh, this and that," my mother's friend is saying. "Frank's got the barbecue going, I'm making some drinks. The girls are gone to the mall."

"Sounds nice," my mother answers. I'm on my back, looking up into the box spring. There's a loop of phone cord resting on my stomach. I watch it rise and fall with my breath.

"How was the concert?"

"Margie, the concert was a disaster. I had him take Patrick down, just something special for them to do together. Dave insisted they leave because the band wasn't doing the songs the way he likes them and then he took Patrick out drinking at some bar with that woman he works with, Marlene. And they get back and Patrick tells me that Dave told her he's had a colonoscopy."

"Is he not well?"

"I don't know, he had a colonoscopy and never breathed a word of it to me but he told some woman from the restaurant."

"You know what, Sharon, I hate to say it but you've got yourself tangled up with a difficult man."

"He's difficult." My mother sighs into the receiver. "The truth is, he exhausts me. I don't know how much longer I'll be at this. Except now I guess he's sick or he might be anyway."

I hear the door to the bedroom open. I bang my head against the box spring and my neck meets with the cold metal of the bed frame. I have to slide out with my shoulders against the floor. I stand up quickly with the receiver in a fist at my waist.

"Were you listening to your mother's phone call?" My father is holding a load of laundry against his chest. "Who's she talking to?"

I drop the receiver into the space moulded to accommodate it and stand up without saying anything. He drops the laundry and it sprawls across the bedspread.

"Get out then, I'm getting dressed." My father picks a pair of dress pants off the pile of laundry and shakes the wrinkles out of them.

Dave

Everyone has their own cash box and their own float and we do the math on a little slip of receipt paper at the end of the night. Me and Marlene always sit in the back booth and do our cashes together.

"Have you talked to Sharon yet?" Marlene asks me, like it's no big deal.

I just shake my head, keep adding things up.

"Why don't you and I have a draw?" she says.

There's a fire escape on the side of the building where we put the garbage out at the end of the night. Drizzle is coming down and leaving pools of water in the wrinkles of the garbage bag. Marlene puts up the hood of her windbreaker and takes the cigarettes out of her pocket.

"You better watch out Sharon doesn't leave you." Marlene takes a draw off the smoke and then she puts it between my lips. Her two fingers are on my lips as I tighten them up to take the cigarette. "At your age, there's only going to be more trips to the doctor from here on out."

Once some hair came loose from Marlene's ponytail and fell in her face when her arms were full of dishes. I saw her blow at the hair, trying to get it out of her eyes, and I put it behind her ear. That's the most that's ever gone on between me and Marlene.

When she lifts her fingers off my lips, I turn my head to exhale and see the car idling in front of the restaurant. Patrick puts a hand on the horn.

"That little frigger." Marlene is laughing. "I'd never blow the horn at my father."

"I've got to get going now." Normally I'd ask if she needed a ride. I toss her cigarette over the balcony.

Patrick

My father collapsed bringing a load of laundry down to

the dryer and had to go into the hospital. My mother and I drive there; I'm holding a plate covered in tinfoil.

"If you bring that dinner in to your father I'll drop you off at Kathy's afterwards," she says. She stays in the car with the radio going while I go up with the plate.

The news is on the TV that swings out over my father's bed. There's a fat paperback with bold letters on the spine on the windowsill.

Dad's lying with the sheet over his face, but when he hears me come in he takes it down.

"The lights in here give me a headache," he says.

I lay the plate on the seat of the chair near his bed.

"You know, this is something that can be avoided," he says. "This is the result of wringing my guts out over whether some missus's appetizer comes out on time, six days a week. The adrenaline from being in that place has rotted me from the inside out. Corroded me, ask your mother. I used to have hair like yours."

I don't unzip my jacket or sit down.

"That's cod au gratin. Mom's waiting in the car—she couldn't find a parking place."

"Your mother doesn't like hospitals."

"She's out in the car."

"You'd better go."

Dave

Carl who does the schedule, his wife sent along flowers with a little square of cardboard sticking up out of them,

"Get Well" written in pen. The whole problem, the whole thing that got my guts in this knot in the first place is that I'm stressed. The job makes me stressed and not working makes me stressed. The only thing close to a solution is winning Lotto 6/49. Or Set for Life. Or Ultimate Dream Home. I never buy a ticket—I mean I buy a few scratch tickets here and there and Sharon does the crosswords but I don't play the lotto like that. I know people pouring half their income into tear-aways. Thinking they're going to be drinking out of coconuts on a resort while someone's remodelling their kitchen. I buy a scratch ticket here or there and sometimes I win enough for a half-case. But I know what they're doing, they're making money. If it wasn't a scam they wouldn't be doing it, it's not a fucking charity.

Sharon's not going to leave me because we're twelve years into a mortgage. I'm lying here wishing I'd said that to Marlene.

Patrick

My nan gave me forty dollars inside a card with a cartoon of a boy leaning against a skateboard. I'm using the money to take Kathy to the movies. We're not allowed to be alone in her house anymore, but I can still go over for dinner. We're not allowed in the basement or her room; if it's not dinnertime we have to sit at the kitchen table or watch TV in the den with her father.

Kathy is painting her nails in the front seat; the smell

of polish flooded the car as soon as she untwisted the lid. My mother will be pissed off if she smells it and figures out that Kathy had polish open in the car.

"What if we hit a pothole?" I ask her at a stoplight.

Kathy squeezes the bottle of polish between her bare knees. She wipes the excess paint off the brush on the inside lip of the bottle.

"I don't mind if it's a little bit messy." She holds her hand up for me to see. "They're already purple, I'm just putting a coat of glitter over it."

I put the window down. The polish looks womanly. I picture her hand gliding up my thigh with all the flecks of glitter catching the light. I slip my hand into my pocket and make sure the money is still there. The five is folded inside the twenty and I rub the two bills together with the hand that isn't on the wheel.

"I'm going to get a job this summer and then I'll take you out all the time. I'll take you to Merl's. Have you been there yet?"

"No, but I really want to go." She waves a glittery hand back and forth in the air, drying the paint. It feels very grown-up having my girlfriend do her nails beside me in the front seat, both of us engulfed in the chemical stink of the polish.

In the lineup to get doughy pretzels Kathy's phone starts buzzing in her purse. She undoes the buckles on the front carefully, trying not to smudge her nails. When she looks at the text she turns her shoulders away from me before answering.

"Who's that?"

"Melissa. Ryan just broke up with her."

We're getting closer to the front of the line.

"What kind of pretzel are you getting?" I'm doing the math in my head, trying to work out the price of the pretzels and the tickets.

"I don't know yet." She's still looking at her phone.

"We're almost at the front of the line."

"She's really upset."

"You better figure out what kind of pretzel you're getting. Or don't. Whatever. I don't care what you do." An unfamiliar nastiness sloshes over my words on their way out of my mouth. I'm afraid there might be a spring of mean impatience gurgling inside me that I didn't know was there.

"I think my dad might be really sick," I say, once we're in the dark of the movie theatre. "He's in the hospital."

"What's wrong with him?" Kathy whispers because the preview music has just started.

"They don't know." It feels good to have said it, but I'm glad we're looking at the screen instead of each other. "Anyway, this is starting."

Dave

I'm going to be in here two or three days at least. The thought of being in this bed for three days gives me anxiety—it's the claustrophobia thing. On airplanes I don't get freaked out thinking the plane is going to crash. It's the tight space, the stale air, all those people crossing and uncrossing their legs, shifting in their chairs, keeping their arms close to their bodies. I hardly drink and when I do it's beer, but on a plane I'll have a stiff drink. I can probably blame my cousin and the trunk incident for that. But I don't know a better feeling than when they broke open the latch on the trunk and lifted the lid. I had tears on my face and everything and I was too old for that but I didn't care. I sat up in the middle of everyone and took a huge breath.

The Hypnotist

ASHLEY WAS TWENTY-SIX and living in her mother's base-ment when her uncle Rob got her an interview for a phar-maceutical representative job. She wasn't qualified for it but he'd pulled strings.

It was at a restaurant with wine glasses and cloth napkins on the tables. The man doing the interview was already there when Ashley arrived; a hostess showed her to his table by the window. He was probably in his early thirties. He had on a white shirt with thin blue lines and a tie. His hair was gelled.

"Ashley, hi. I'm Martin Dove, nice to meet you." He held out his hand and she could tell this was the kind of job where they expected you to be well-manicured and charming.

Her uncle Rob had given her a package of pamph-lets to review for the meeting. The drug was an early treatment for uterine fibroids. She had googled uterine fibroids. She looked at pictures of hard white keloids on a soft, red uterine wall. She read most of the Wikipedia page on uterine fibroids and skimmed the pamphlets. It wasn't clear how much she was expected to know for the interview.

The waitress came over with menus. Martin Dove asked for a coffee, so Ashley ordered one too.

"I'm going to be upfront with you. You're not really qualified for this job. I'm doing this as a favour to your uncle, who helped me out when I was starting. If you blow my socks off the job is yours—but you're up against people with experience in the field."

"Okay," Ashley said.

"Let's take a minute to look at the menu before we begin," Martin Dove said.

The cheapest things on the menu were close to thirty dollars.

"I'm definitely going to try an appetizer," he said. "What about you?"

She wondered if he'd had his teeth bleached.

"It all looks pretty heavy, I think I'll skip it." She tried to sound upbeat.

"Okay, let's get down to it. You approach the doctor and ask him or her if they have a moment. If they say yes, you do a seven-minute pitch; if they say they're too busy, offer to walk with them, take the elevator with them; if they agree to that, you do a two-and-a-half-minute pitch. I'm going to do both for you and then I'll let you give it a try. Your uncle said he passed along the pamphlets?"

Ashley took the pamphlets out of her purse and laid them on the table. Martin Dove took out his cell phone and turned on the timer.

They were there for three hours. The only other customer was an old man who ordered a steak and read a woodworking magazine. He was sat behind the man interviewing her and she could tell he was eavesdropping.

Ashley couldn't get the spiel out fast enough. When she did finish before the timer she missed information or got the facts wrong. The more she stumbled over her words the more flustered she became. The steak man had left and the waitress had taken their dishes and kept passive-aggressively offering them more coffee. It reminded her of when her father tried to teach her to drive a standard. She'd gotten stuck near the top of a gentle hill with a car behind her. The clutch screamed every time she tried to change into second gear and the car slid a little closer to the vehicle behind her while the driver laid on the horn. Eventually her father wrenched the handbrake up and they ran around outside the car, switching seats. When he got behind the wheel, the car flew silently over the crest and she hated herself.

"It's not easy," Martin Dove told her. She had the feeling he was hitting on her but he smiled so warmly at the waitress that it was hard to tell. "Okay, the two things you need to work on are being confident and being concise. I'm just going to run to the washroom, you read through the material and you can give it another go when I get back."

Ashley was tempted to leave while he was in the bathroom. The waitress dumped the ice tray into the sink behind the bar. The two young women made eye contact as the sound of the ice cubes crashing into stainless steel bounced around the almost-empty room. Martin Dove came back from the washroom and waited at the bar for the waitress to turn around. She was startled by him and dropped the empty tray on the floor.

"We're not keeping you, are we?" Ashley heard him say. He stooped and picked up the tray.

"Take your time."

"Do you close before dinner?" He had his elbow on the counter and he was leaning toward the waitress.

"Take your time," the girl said again, settling the ice tray back into the top of the cooler.

"YOU'RE LUCKY YOU didn't get that job," her mother said. "It would be lots of money but it's not right, those drug companies just want to make money."

"Everyone just wants to make money. Any job I have is going to be to make money," Ashley said.

"What about going to CONA for cooking, remember when you were talking about that?"

"That was like two years ago."

"What's for dinner?" Ashley's sister Vicky had come up from the basement.

Ashley's phone buzzed on the kitchen table. It was an email from Martin Dove.

"I got an email from the pharmaceutical company," Ashley said.

"They want you now?" her mother asked.

Vicky opened the fridge.

Hi Ashley,

I hope this isn't too forward.

I'd like to take you to a non-work-related dinner.

Best,

Martin

"He's asking me out."

"Who?" her mother asked. "I'm not making dinner, your father's going to be at work late tonight. There's a can of chicken noodle soup there if you want."

"The man who interviewed me. He was really handsome."

"Oh, for Jesus' sake. No. Do you see what happened? He wanted to ask you out so he gave the job to someone else."

"No, he was really nice. I did a terrible job, seriously, I was tripping all over my words."

"Don't date that man, Ashley, do you hear me? He fucked you over," her mother said.

"Mom, he didn't. I was bad at it and I wasn't qualified. There were more qualified candidates."

"According to who, Ashley?"

"He sounds like a sleazebag to me," Vicky said.

"Nobody asked your opinion, it's none of your business."

"Where's the can opener?" Vicky asked, holding up the tin of soup. "Is this the add-water kind?"

"Read the label, you moron," Ashley said.

"I thought you were smarter than this, Ashley," her mother said.

"Also, the rabbit stinks, you need to clean the cage." Ashley put her mug in the dishwasher.

Kevin, one of Vicky's ex-boyfriends, had bought her a rabbit for Valentine's Day. It had been living in a cage in the furnace room for a year and a half. The furnace room didn't have a door and you could smell the rabbit's piss and shit in the downstairs hallway. It was mean, it bared its big teeth if you put your hand out. If Vicky forgot to clean the cage, you could smell it through the whole house.

THEY WENT TO a different restaurant downtown. Martin ordered white wine and the waitress brought a bucket filled with ice for the bottle to sit in.

"I bought us tickets to a show after dinner. But we don't have to go, only if you feel like it." He lifted the wine out of the vase and topped up her glass even though she'd only had a single mouthful. The sides of the bottle glistened with melted ice. "It's Reveen, have you heard of him?"

"He's a singer?" Ashley took a breadstick out of a bowl in the centre of the table and swirled it in a little dish of vinegar and oil.

"He's a hypnotist. It's a little hokey, but I thought it'd be fun. No pressure, honestly."

"I'll go."

"This guy is world famous. He's on a world tour right now but he loves Newfoundland. This is actually the son of the original Reveen — Reveen died recently. I've never seen his son but I've heard he's good. Do you know what you want?" Martin closed his menu and laid it on the edge of the table.

"Do you have to be hypnotized?" She laid her menu on top of his.

"He chooses volunteers from the audience. People volunteer, you don't have to do it if you don't want to. I've been twice and both times I said I was going to do it and chickened out at the last minute."

"What does he make people do?"

"Oh you'll see, it's very funny."

Halfway through her shellfish pasta, she went to the bathroom. Partly just to see what the bathroom was like. She texted Vicky and told her about the hypnotist while she was peeing.

Omg lame, he sounds so weird!

Ashley pressed the button on top of her phone and made the screen turn black. Vicky hadn't dated anyone in almost a year. A couple of weeks ago Kevin showed up at four in the morning on a Wednesday, drunk out of his mind and fucked on coke. He and Vicky had been broken up for months. He rang the doorbell three times, then went around back and punched a hole in the low, little window to Vicky's basement bedroom. Their father called the cops. The red and blue lights swung around, drenching the white house in colour and then swooping away. The whole family watched through the living room window as the cop led Kevin away from the side of the house with blood running down his sleeve. When the cops left, their father went to bed and their mother made a pot of Sleepytime tea.

"What a fucking moron," Ashley said when they were all gathered at one end of the kitchen table with their mugs.

"Maybe we shouldn't have called the cops. Now he'll have a record." Vicky's eyes were swollen from crying.

"We had to call the police, Vicky, he could have been trying to hurt you for all we know," their mother said. "You know what else, that fucking rabbit has to go. I'm not having it in my house. It can go to the SPCA."

"I'm going to clean the cage tomorrow, Dad took me to get hay yesterday," Vicky said.

"You should sleep on the couch, your bedroom will be freezing with the window busted."

THEY GOT A cab to the Arts and Culture Centre and Martin paid for it. After he got his change he handed the cab driver a ten-dollar bill as a tip. Ashley hadn't been to the Arts and Culture Centre since the sixth grade, when her whole school had gone to see *Alice in Wonderland: The Musical*. She had fallen asleep before the end of the play but she'd loved the costumes. The girl who'd played Alice had yellow-blond hair that went all the way to her ankles. Remembering the play now, Ashley realized for the first time that it must have been a wig.

The lobby was packed. They waited in a long line to get to a counter where Martin said his name and a middle-aged woman handed him two tickets.

"Thank you so much, I have to say that's a beautiful brooch," Martin told the woman.

"You like it?" The woman looked down at the brooch, smiling. "My daughter gave me that four years ago."

"It's beautiful." Martin waved the tickets at her. "Thank you, very crowded here tonight, you're doing a great job."

Ashley felt a hand on her arm. It was her aunt Tracey, with uncle Gord. They were both holding programs with "Reveen: The Next Generation" printed above the face of a man in a black suit with sequins sewn on the lapels.

"Ashley, who's this handsome young man you're with? I don't think we've been introduced."

Martin smiled as though Ashley's aunt was being very funny.

"This is Martin," Ashley told them. She found she was proud to introduce him, to be seen with him.

"So you're fans of Reveen?" her uncle asked. "Myself and Tracey go see him every time he's here."

"This is my third time, my father loves the show," Martin said.

"Now, I don't know if he's going to be able to do what his father did — his father knew how to work a crowd, he was a very funny man." Uncle Gord was talking and aunt Tracey was nodding.

"That's what everyone's here to find out," Martin said. Ashley found herself nodding.

They faced the stage, sidestepping along the aisle to their seats. When they were settled in the dark with their programs in their laps, Martin leaned close to her ear.

"I've been meaning to tell you, you look very pretty tonight." His lips were touching her hair. She could see the bald spot on the back of uncle Gord's head two rows in front of them.

"Thank you." She could count on one hand the number of times she'd been called pretty since puberty. Men were always telling her she had a great ass and her friends always complimented her hair, but Vicky was prettier. Vicky had a nose so tiny and delicate it looked like it had been sculpted out of marzipan.

When the lights went down she laid her left hand on the armrest, hoping he would take it. The hypnotist stood on a stage lined with chairs. He explained that not everyone was susceptible to hypnosis.

"I'm looking for volunteers," the hypnotist told the audience, gesturing to the empty chairs. "This is an opportunity to find your inner performer, to showcase talents you may not even know you have."

"Do you want to go? You should go if you want to," Ashley whispered to Martin.

"I want to be with you." He took her hand and a jolt travelled through it straight to her crotch. A man next to them jumped up and they had to stand to let him pass on his way to the stage.

"No one will be humiliated in this show. This is clean, family entertainment." The hypnotist waved people up with wide sweeps of his arm.

With the help of two ushers, fifteen volunteers were seated in a semi-circle on the stage.

"You are now entering a state of deep relaxation," said the son of Reveen, speaking into a microphone. "I want you to imagine there is a helium balloon tied to your index finger, gently tugging it up into the air."

"Here we go." Martin squeezed her hand.

Ashley watched as the volunteers' index fingers wiggled, then rose slowly until they were pointing at the ceiling. Their faces were expressionless. Their arms were completely straight. Martin was leaning forward in his seat at an awkward angle to see over the shoulder of a tall man in front of him. Ashley looked to the right to see how the woman next to her was reacting and saw her own finger pointed straight up, level with her ear. She took her hand down and stuck it in her pocket.

All around her, people's index fingers were straightening out and moving toward the ceiling at varying speeds. Everyone was staring at the stage. Martin's left hand was resting on his knee and she saw that a finger was raised.

Next the hypnotist had the volunteers do a conga line

around the stage. People were laughing hysterically all around her. She angled her phone so the light mostly shone into the seat to check the time. They had already been there for almost two hours. Martin was completely engrossed. Her hand was sweating inside of his but she didn't move it. She could make out uncle Gord's outline ahead of them; he was shaking with laughter. She shifted her hips back and forth, wiggling the stiffness out of her lower back.

After the show, the wine buzz had worn off and left her tired. They waited for their cab in the concrete tunnel that enclosed the doors to the lobby. A wave of people was pouring out of the building, causing congestion on the squat set of stairs outside the entrance. Inside the lobby a man with a camera and a large microphone was interviewing members of the audience for an ad that would be posted on the Reveen web site. Uncle Gord was gesticulating into the camera and aunt Tracey was nodding along.

"Does Danazil work?" Ashley asked Martin.

"You saw the numbers." He said it curtly. She had never seen him be cold before but found she wasn't surprised by it.

"I mean, do you think it's better than other drugs? Do you think it's the best choice?" If there was a nasty side of him she wanted it to worm its way to the surface.

"Everything has side effects. I think that's our cab." Just as he said it a teenager in a polka-dot rain jacket ran out of the lobby. The girl held the cab door open for her slow-moving mother.

"Would you take it? If you weren't a guy? Would you have your mom take it?"

"I don't want to talk about work right now." He sounded like a teacher telling his class to be quiet. Three cabs pulled up at once and Martin strode over to the first one and opened the back door.

She looked at her house as they pulled up to it. Her parents would be in bed. Her sister was probably watching TV in the living room, wrapped in a comforter. The rabbit would be grunting and snuffling its way around the cage in the lonely furnace room.

She leaned in and kissed him on the cheek.

"We'll go for dinner again?" he asked. She was already half out of the cab.

"Sure," she said, in a way that let him know she didn't mean it.

A couple of nights later, her mother called her into the living room. Vicky was curled on the couch with a mug of Pepsi and a plate of chicken fingers. There was a bright splotch of ketchup on her plate.

"That's the one you went to see, isn't it?" Her mother was watching the news from her recliner.

The hypnotist was standing behind a woman in a furry leopard-print jacket and leopard-print hat. She wore Elton John sunglasses with see-through rims.

"That's the wife," her mother explained. "See, they're donating his suit." Her mother pointed at the TV.

"My husband always loved Newfoundland, we have so many great memories of our time here," Reveen's wife was saying. Ashley was surprised that she had a British accent. Reveen's wife put a hand under one of the reflective lenses of her sunglasses to wipe a tear away.

"That's the mother of the guy I saw," Ashley said. "That's him behind her, the son of Reveen."

She didn't remember the hypnotist having an accent. He was standing behind his mother, nodding along to her speech. When his mother finished talking, the hypnotist pulled a black sheet off a glass case. The torso of a mannequin filled the chest of the red tuxedo but the legs and arms hung empty. This suit was more much elegant than what the hypnotist had been wearing when she saw him perform.

"We should go see the suit," Ashley said. "It'll be free to go see it, it looks like it'll just be on display in the lobby."

The news moved on to a story about drug dogs finding marijuana in a locker at Brother Rice Junior High.

"We just saw it," her mother said.

Sightings

A GROUP OF WOMEN in jean shorts and bubblegum-pink T-shirts with "Bachelorette" in fat white cursive over their breasts were making their way down the street. The bride-to-be had a plastic tiara and a boa that was shedding feathers. The hot pink feathers floated in the women's backdraft as they lurched down George Street.

It was Kayla's first bachelorette and she barely knew most of these women. Half of them had flown out from Alberta, where her brother had been living for the past three years. There was a party at a house in Cowan Heights beforehand. They did jello shots out of little plastic cups—the same kind that Kayla filled with ketchup for people who requested it with their French toast when she worked brunch.

There was a game where you had to hold a cucumber between your thighs and pass it to someone else, who took it from you by clamping their own thighs around it. The point of the game was to create this awkward moment where your breasts were almost touching and you were looking into each other's eyes with this phallic thing between both of your jean-short-clad crotches. Kayla successfully passed a cucumber to her future sister-in-law, Debbie, who she'd met for the first time at the airport that morning. Then she hid in the bathroom for twenty minutes.

Kayla had done a bit of the East Coast Trail, the chunk that starts up by Fort Amherst, a few days before her brother got in from Alberta. It was a grey day, cold for July—most people were wearing pants and long sleeves—but she went anyway because it was her first day off in two weeks and she had been planning to do it for months.

She ended up being glad to have gone on a cool day because there was no one around. The only people she saw were two men on mountain bikes in helmets and reflective sunglasses. She had to step into a bush to let them career past.

She saw a pond from the trail and worked her way down a mucky path to a little cement platform. On the platform, she looked around for hikers on the hills above the pond. Although she was surrounded by woods, she could hear the wail of an ambulance sailing down from Shea Heights. She hadn't seen anyone since the mountain bikers though, and they'd been travelling in the opposite direction. She stripped and lowered herself into the pond.

The water was warm, considering the summer they'd had. She was dreading the wedding: the effort of being welcoming to in-laws she'd never met; of dressing up, making small talk, telling everyone she didn't have any plans for when she finished university. But alone in the middle of the pond, she felt excited to be seeing her brother soon.

She dried off with her T-shirt and then put the damp top back on. The sound of the ambulance had made her want to get deeper into the woods. Her wet hair dripped on her shoulders. Most of the trail was very clearly marked with pink gravel and little signs; there were narrow board-walks in the places where the path took you into bog. But a couple of times she became disoriented and had to back-track to find where she'd strayed off the path.

She found herself on a flat stretch of land with humps of yellow-grey rock rising out of moss. About ten feet ahead of her she saw a medium-sized dog standing on a small hill. She listened for its owner. The animal stared at her; it was caramel-coloured with a fluffy mane and a wolf's face. It was a coyote. She had seen lots of photos of coyotes on Facebook — dead ones, strapped to the backs of Ski-Doos — when the government first started paying people for their coats. The animal turned and ran into the woods.

She thought of the woman in Nova Scotia who'd been mauled to death by a pack of coyotes and realized that she had no reception up there. Even if she had reception, it would take anyone she called a long time to get to her. But she wanted a picture. She turned the phone's camera on and walked toward the hill the wild dog had disappeared over. She got to the top, her phone held out in front of her, the screen a digital blur of pine needles.

AT MIDNIGHT THEY called cabs to take them downtown. Kayla sat in the back seat with her brother's fiancée. Debbie took Kayla's hand and squeezed it.

"Who's getting married?" the cab driver asked, making eye contact in the rear-view. Debbie let go of Kayla's hand so she could raise it like she was in school.

"So this is the last hurrah?" he said.

"I sure hope not." Debbie flung the tail of the boa over her shoulder. The synthetic feathers brushed Kayla's cheek.

"I don't mind if you smoke as long as you put the windows down, seeing as it's your special night."

The windows went down on either side of the car and the women got cigarettes out of their purses.

One of the girls saw her boyfriend go inside Karaoke Krazy so they all joined a long line outside. After paying cover some of them headed for the bathroom and some of them started shouldering their way through the tightly packed crowd around the bar.

Someone behind Kayla stumbled and pushed her face-first into the T-shirt of a man who reeked of cologne. The zipper of his windbreaker scratched her cheek.

"I'm sorry." Kayla backed up.

"Hey, don't worry about it." The man put a big hand on her lower back. Kayla looked around her; she saw the back of one of the Barbie-convertible-pink shirts in a throng leaning against the bar. She tried to move away from the man but he grabbed her hip and pulled her into him.

"Hey, slow down, tell me about your T-shirt, who's getting married?"

There was barely room to move; it was loud and no one was watching them. Kayla dug her elbow into the man's fatty side and pushed herself away from him. She kept pushing until she was out of the bar. The man's cologne had been overwhelming and she wanted fresh air.

When she got into the street she saw the man had followed her outside.

"Hey, want a cigarette?"

Kayla started walking quickly toward Water Street. She was planning to get a cab; she would text Debbie and tell her she'd gone home. The man was following a few paces behind her.

"You don't have to be rude," he was calling to her.

A clutch of people standing around a hot dog vendor laughed at the man as he lurched drunkenly down the street after her.

Kayla closed her hand around her phone in her purse. When she got to Water Street it was empty. The man was still behind her so she kept walking down the dark, empty street.

"Hey, slow down, I'm just trying to talk to you."

Kayla wheeled around and held her phone in front of her.

"I'm filming you."

He turned and started back toward George Street, yelling insults into the night.

All Good, Having a Great Time

ALL MELISSA'S RELATIVES called to tell her they'd seen her picture at the mall and she looked beautiful. It was her first modelling job, with Emerald Basics, a chain store that did window advertisements featuring local girls for each of their locations. She'd modelled a back-to-school look, a knapsack slung over one shoulder. A life-sized photo of her was hung in the window of the local store with "Back To School Blow-Out Sale" written on the side.

When the company asked if she'd be interested in doing a national campaign, her mother hosted a barbecue and invited the family to come celebrate. After Melissa wrote her high school finals, the company flew her to Montreal and rented her a hotel room for two weeks.

The hotel was surrounded by big box stores. She drew back the screechy blinds to reveal a view of skinny sidewalks and massive parking lots. Her mother told her to get taxis to the photo shoots, but she crossed the four-lane road and bought a toothbrush at Walmart so she could ask the cashier how to get to a bus or the subway. The woman drew her a map to the Longueuil metro station on the back of her receipt.

She met Ruth at the photo shoot. Ruth's hair and eyebrows were bleached white. She was three years older than Melissa. Her eyes were very green.

"This is a hard shoot," Melissa said. "Do you think?"

"Worth it though. Emerald Basics pay pretty well and if they like you they'll ask you back," Ruth said. "What're you doing after this?"

When the shoot finished it was nighttime. Melissa felt like she had just come out of an afternoon movie to find it dark outside. Ruth bought them each a flask of vodka; she got ID'd at the cash. Melissa stood sheepishly at her side.

"I know a party we can go to but it won't start for a while," Ruth said. "Do you want to drink in the park for a bit?"

They sat at a picnic table and watched people jog around a man-made lake. A few feet away from them a group of boys in denim vests were drinking from tall cans. The boys kept calling to them, inviting them over.

"Should we sit with them? They might give us beer," Ruth said.

"No." Melissa felt embarrassed by how quickly and vehemently she answered. "Unless you want to."

"Nah." Ruth dropped her empty flask into a metal garbage bin nestled against the picnic table. "Let's go to the party."

Ruth took her to an apartment that people rented for after-parties. A guy in a grey hoodie and skinny jeans sat inside the front door with a cash box.

"Twenty bucks. If you leave you might not get back in." Even in the porch the music was deafening. Melissa had sixty dollars in cash in her small hemp wallet. Ruth's wallet was made of shiny black pleather.

There was no furniture except for a kitchen table where the DJ had set up. The windows had garbage bags duct-taped over them. Ruth was still wearing her makeup from the shoot, bright pink lipstick and shimmering blush. Melissa wished she hadn't washed hers off. Jackets were piled in a room in the front of the apartment and people were passed out on them.

"That's my friend Laura." Ruth dropped her coat on a girl in a bikini top and acid-wash jean shorts. "Keep your wallet on you."

People were doing coke off the kitchen counter. Everyone knew Ruth. They touched her hair and praised her lipstick. As soon as she introduced Melissa to anyone, they hugged her and offered her a drink. Melissa felt her phone vibrating in her pocket. She knew it was her mother, calling to ask about the shoot, but she ignored it.

"Let's pee before there's a lineup." Ruth took her hand and led her into a hallway. They both swallowed a pinch of MDMA inside a scrap of twisted-up toilet paper in the bathroom. It was only the second time she'd done it but when Ruth lifted the little white bundle to Melissa's lips she opened her mouth for it without hesitating. When they got out of the bathroom a new wave of people had arrived and space was shrinking. To move through a room you had to wriggle through the crowd.

The next morning Melissa woke up on the couch in Ruth's apartment. She was still dressed. Her book bag was on the floor next to her and when she unzipped the front pouch she saw her wallet was there.

She went to the kitchen and drank from the tap. There were thirteen texts from her mother but she was too hungover to answer them. The door to Ruth's bedroom was open.

"Ruth?" She leaned over Ruth and spoke quietly. "Ruth? I'm going to go."

Ruth opened her eyes but kept her head flat on the pillow. Pink lipstick was smeared across her cheek.

"What time is it?"

"It's really early. Thanks for having me."

"Don't go, I hate being alone when I'm hungover. I'll get up." Ruth flicked the blanket off. She was wearing a baggy T-shirt and underwear. "Actually, let's just lie down for another minute."

"HE'S A PERFORMANCE artist, but he makes money as a cam boy and he does some domination stuff for like lawyers and businessmen." They were going to visit a friend of Ruth's to get pot to numb their hangovers.

"Like what?" Melissa asked. They were on the platform waiting for the metro to pull up.

"He has one client who pretends to be his footstool. Ken just gets naked and puts his feet up on the guy for an hour and watches movies on his laptop."

Warm air rushed through the tunnel as the train pulled in, for a moment Melissa thought she might throw up.

"Ken is like the sweetest person ever. When I had the flu he made me chicken soup, like from scratch. He made the broth from a chicken he cooked himself. This is our stop coming up," Ruth said as they pulled into Parc metro station.

When they arrived at Ken's, Ruth said, "Melissa was just asking me what kind of domination stuff you do." Melissa blushed and felt betrayed.

Ken held his hand out for her to shake. He had huge windows with a view of the parking lot of a chandelier warehouse.

Melissa went to the bathroom and quickly texted her mother.

All good, having a great time, will call later.

She felt the phone vibrate with a response immediately but she didn't check it.

Melissa and Ruth sat on the edge of a futon and smoked a joint while Ken made them waffles. "Ken, that's Riley!" Ruth's voice was shrill and Melissa's hangover made her feel it in the back of her eyeballs. She winced.

Ruth hopped off the futon and tapped the big plate-glass window. A girl was walking along the opposite side of the street with headphones on.

"She lives across the street." Ken was pouring a ladleful of waffle batter into a waffle maker.

"That little bitch." Ruth sat back down and passed Melissa the joint.

"Oh, get over it." Ken closed the lid of the waffle maker and batter sizzled out of the sides and dripped onto the counter.

"She's a pretentious little bitch," Ruth said to Melissa.

Melissa felt exhausted, the smell of the waffles cooking was making her sick. She couldn't understand how Ruth was summoning so much intensity.

"You were like in love with her six months ago," Ken said. He looked at Melissa and added, "They used to be best friends. They lived together."

"Well, that was before I realized what a pretentious little bitch she is," Ruth said. "I can't stand people who don't know how to have fun."

When Ruth finished her waffles the girls walked to the metro station. Melissa could feel the tightness of sunburn surfacing on her cheeks.

"I need to figure out how to get back to the hotel from here," Melissa said when they arrived.

"Why don't you just come stay at my place? There's a mattress in the spare room."

"You wouldn't mind?"

"Stay with me."

Once they were through the turnstiles, Melissa felt her appetite returning and bought a two-dollar slice of cheese pizza.

"I don't want to go home," Melissa said. She was holding the greasy paper plate in her lap.

"Don't. Move in with me. You can live in my closet room for like a hundred and fifty bucks a month. Ken did for a while."

A man's voice said the name of each metro station over a loudspeaker as they pulled into it. Melissa used the names to trace the path they were making across the map on the wall of the train. She tried to memorize the pronunciation of each one.

Ruth set her up in the closet room before going to bed. The room was just wide enough for a mattress. The only other furniture was a lamp with fat plastic jewels and brass flowers.

"See, this is cozy! I had a room this size before," Ruth said. "You should just live here."

Melissa wondered if this was the apartment Ruth had shared with the girl she'd seen through the window at Ken's. Was this the girl's lamp? Melissa plugged the brown cord into the wall and clicked the lamp on. There was no shade and the light from the bare bulb made her reflection appear in the window.

The next day Melissa left the apartment early in the morning. She had googled Internet cafés in the area the night before on her phone. She'd seen a Street View image of a squat white building with bars on the window that was open 24/7. It was eight in the morning but it was already hot.

At the counter she paid for an hour, and then extra to rent a set of headphones. The guy at the counter looked about thirty and he had a Poké Ball tattooed on the middle of his neck, covering his Adam's apple. He spoke to her in French first but switched to English when he saw the look on her face.

"I just got this done before work last night, it'll look better when the swelling goes down," he said, noticing her staring at his neck.

"It looks great," Melissa said.

"You're into retro games and stuff?" The guy was taking her in with new interest.

"Not really, I mean not especially. I just think it looks cool, the colours are great," Melissa said too quickly.

"Did you want headphones with a mic in them? It's an extra four bucks for ones with the mic." The guy swung around and lifted a pair of headphones off a cup hook that was screwed into the wall behind him.

When the call connected Melissa shrunk the Skype window; she didn't like that anyone passing behind her seat could see her mother smiling into the webcam.

"I want to stay in Montreal," Melissa said, speaking quietly into a microphone in the cord of the headphones. "I'm moving here."

"That's something to think about," her mother said.

"I already thought about it." Melissa could see herself in a small window at the bottom of the screen. She was aware of how foolish she looked with the puffy leather earmuffs of the rented headphones framing her face.

"You're going to have to talk to your father, he's at bowling. I'm sure he would say that what you need to be thinking about right now is a long-term plan," her mother said. "This modelling stuff is great for now but it isn't going to be an option in five or ten years."

Melissa glanced over her shoulder and saw the guy at the counter leaning on his elbows, surveying the room. He smiled at her, absently dragging his fingers over the new tattoo.

"I know that," Melissa whispered into the microphone.

"Can you speak up?" her mother asked.

"I have money, I'm staying here," Melissa said, suddenly overwhelmed with the need to get out of the dimly lit room.

THERE WERE BURSTS of money when she or Ruth got a modelling gig and they lived extravagantly until they were suddenly broke. They all but shared a bank account. They bought each other's weed and groceries and drinks at the bar. When they were out of money they worked, but as little as possible. Ruth did three-hour shifts handing out samples at the liquor store. Melissa worked two days a week at the Dollarama around the corner from their house.

It was hot. They smoked weed and went swimming. When they had money they went to a hotel on Ste-Catherine. They rode the air-conditioned elevator to the pool on the roof. Pool attendants sweating in suit jackets would drape clean towels over lounge chairs that overlooked the city as they stepped out of the pool.

When they didn't have money they spent their afternoons in the shallow end of the Parc Jarry pool. They watched people hula-hooping in the scabby grass outside the chain-link fence. They could see the picnic bench where they'd gotten drunk together the first time. Melissa was always pointing this out to Ruth.

They'd hold the edge of the pool, their backs facing the sun, feet lightly splashing on the surface. Ruth would tell Melissa about the sex she'd had the night before. Ruth and Ken always stayed out later than Melissa. Ruth brought guys home. The rhythmic knocking and moaning would wake Melissa up and she felt like she'd never known anyone so well in her life.

Sometimes Melissa and Ruth got drunk in the morning.

"Hair of the dog," Ruth announced, pouring Jameson out of a twenty-sixer into matching Couche-Tard mugs Melissa had found in a box of dishes on the sidewalk. They drank the liquor with flat ginger ale on the balcony. They watched their Greek neighbours pruning the lemon tree they'd planted in the small square lawn in front of their door.

There was a sale on frozen shrimp rings and they bought ten. When they got to the checkout, two stacks of shrimp rings and a miniature rose bush from the gardening section were the only things in their cart. It was eleven in the morning, and the cashier scrunched her face up when she smelled the alcohol on Melissa's breath.

"What a bitch," Ruth said, walking through the sliding doors into the morning with the rose bush in her arms.

The tiny blossoms were getting tangled in her hair.

"I guess." Melissa was following her with a plastic bag of shrimp rings in each hand.

There were several days that summer when the only thing they ate was a shrimp ring defrosted and shared on the balcony. There was a small tub of marinara sauce in the centre of each ring. They piled the slippery, shucked shells into a teacup.

Melissa had started going to free yoga classes in the basement of a church around the corner from the apartment. One evening she came back to Ken and Ruth doing lines of coke on the coffee table in the living room.

"Melissa!" Ruth jumped up off the living room floor. "We've been waiting for you. Do a line with us."

"No thanks, I'm all relaxed from yoga." Melissa propped her yoga mat up in the corner of the living room.

"Miss Yogi over there." The mirror from the bathroom was resting on the couch and Ken was parting his hair in it. "I wonder what Miss Yogi is going to do with her five thousand dollars?"

"We have something to tell you." Ruth was giggling on her back on the living room floor, kicking her legs in the air.

"You two are fucked."

Ken had gotten the three of them a gig. He was sleeping with some big-deal casting director who got them in on a catalogue shoot coming up in Montreal.

Melissa Skyped her parents on Ruth's laptop, sitting on the edge of the bathtub because the bathroom was the quietest and most private room in the apartment.

"Melissa, you should put that money away for school," her mother said. Her brother had just gotten two kittens and one was walking along the back of the couch behind her mother's head. Melissa could see its hips waggle from side to side.

"Which kitten is that?"

Her mother tilted her head to look at the cat.

"Pop-Tart. You need to start thinking about how you handle your money. Talk to your father, he'll have good advice for you."

Melissa could hear her brother trying to rap along to music in the background.

"You could say congratulations."

"I'm very happy for you, Melissa," her mother said.

"I have to go now, we're going out for lunch." Melissa closed the lid of the computer before her mother could say anything else.

MELISSA WAS A snail. Her dress had a hard plastic shell sewn on to its back. The shell was see-through with orange satin curled inside it. A stylist pulled a hood out of the shell where it met Melissa's neck and snuggled it over the top of her head. The hairdresser stuck a cool metal comb into the hood and coaxed Melissa's curls out around the edges of it.

"What do you think?" Both women stepped back to look at her. The hairdresser lifted her coffee off the workstation behind her.

"I fucking love that hood. I want hooded everything now," the hairdresser said.

"It's working, what you did with the curls is really working," the stylist said.

"Don't tilt your head too much, the hood will slide down very easily and then we'll have to get your hair done again."

The set was framed by two glass walls that met to make a corner. They were slicked with emerald green goo. Lights were playing on the walls to make it look like the set was underwater. The floor was covered in pink and baby blue gravel. There were eight-foot replicas of plastic aquarium plants in bright pink and light blue with silver sparkles.

"You're captured sea goddesses," the director told the girls as they walked on set. "The designer was inspired by learning that ninety percent of the fish in tropical tanks are not bred in captivity. You used to live in the wild and now you're cramped in this tank. You're depressed, lethargic, yearning for the ocean. Can you give me that?"

Melissa nodded gently, careful not to dislodge the hood. The other girls' dresses were meant to evoke fish; metal fins were attached to the curves of their waists and asses. They had pale blue lipstick and iridescent blush on their cheeks.

The girls couldn't cross the gravel in their heels so they were carried across in the arms of set managers and lighting techs. Melissa was last to go. The other six girls had to be locked into harnesses and lifted into the air.

She waited at the edge of the set. The shell was heavy; her back was aching from it. There were rough edges that chafed her bare shoulders. She thought about the money.

Ruth was the first fish to be jerked into the air.

"Bring her down a couple inches, I want her to interact with the plant," the photographer called from behind the camera. Ruth was lowered into the branches of a hot pink fern. She laid her cheek on a plastic leaf and relaxed her face. There were silver streaks in Ruth's dress that reflected the pink of the fern.

"I love that, perfect, disaffected, you've been wrenched from your wild, exciting life in the sea, I'm feeling it, arch your back a little to emphasize the fin," the director called to Ruth. Melissa felt herself flood with jealousy. Ruth twisted her body and the plastic fern shivered as though it was moving in a current of water.

"This is why I fought for real plants, we couldn't get this kind of interaction if we Photoshopped them in afterwards," the photographer said, leaning toward the director. "Okay, let's get everyone else up there."

While the other girls were being raised in the air, the director told a lighting tech to carry Melissa to a rock at the edge of the tank. The lighting tech was a muscular Cuban man, shorter than Melissa. He hooked one arm under her knees and the other cradled her lower back. When he took a step the shell bounced and knocked her in the back of the head.

"Watch the shell," the director yelled.

The man lowered her onto a three-foot-tall plastic rock

with some small neon ferns sticking out of it.

"You need to communicate 'snail.' Let your body suction to the rock, make sure you're selling the shell, I want the side of the shell to the camera for the whole shoot. Just imagine what it's like to have that suction the whole length of your body."

Once all the girls were in position, a technician walked backward with a rake, smoothing the stones. They took photographs for six hours. Melissa was lying across the rock with her toes touching the gravel and her back arched; after the first forty-five minutes her calf muscles were quivering.

In the dressing room Ruth showed her two purple stripes across her rib cage where the harness had been digging into it.

When the money came through, Melissa paid off her credit card so she could book a trip. She wanted to go on a trip that involved rainforests and swimming in lagoons but Ruth wanted to go to a city.

"I want to eat in fancy restaurants and go to nightclubs." Ruth was ripping apart the packaging of a three-hundred-dollar blender she'd just brought home on the metro with her.

"You should keep all that stuff, in case it doesn't work. Do you have the receipt?" Melissa asked.

"Do you always have to be such a fucking drag?" Ruth stuffed the box into their already overflowing garbage.

They booked a seventies camper trailer in a junkyard in Brooklyn from Airbnb. It was connected to a warehouse that was some kind of communal artist space. The blurb asked that guests let the owners know if they were uncomfortable with nudity.

"You're kidding," Ruth said when Melissa suggested they get the bus down. "We're definitely not getting the bus. I'm planning to get very drunk on the plane."

"I don't want to waste money just for the sake of it. The bus will end up being faster if you think of all the time it'll take us to get to and from the airport." Melissa didn't care that much about how they got there but it suddenly felt very important not to back down.

"I guess I'm getting drunk by myself on an airplane." Ruth was cross-legged in her bed, watching TV on her laptop.

"I guess it's not that much cheaper, really," Melissa tried. "If we booked the plane tickets now."

"Don't worry about it. We'll just meet up in Brooklyn." Ruth pushed down a button on the keyboard, making the actors' voices blare out of the tinny computer speakers.

THE OVERNIGHT BUS was cold and Melissa had to point her knees into the aisle at an uncomfortable angle to avoid touching the girl in the window seat. At the border she remembered that the Airbnb guy had messaged them and said not to tell the cops or anyone else in a "position of authority" that they were paying to stay in the junkyard.

A customs officer got on the bus and spoke through a microphone that clipped onto his shirt. He told everyone to leave their bags on their seats and file into the customs office in an orderly fashion. When all the passengers were off, border guards let muscular dogs run down the centre aisle of the bus.

The customs office was just a short cinder-block building with a glass wall facing the parking lot and a narrow walkway around it. Inset lights shone out of the cement overhang of the roof, lighting up the outside of the building. Guards were hauling bags out of the bottom of the bus and flinging them onto the pavement. A pair of dogs leapt into the underbelly of the bus.

Melissa knew "Where will you be staying?" was a question they always asked. A guard approached all the young, non-white men one by one and asked them to step into a cubicle. The guard had close-cropped hair and big muscles. He was gruff and showy about leading the men into the room.

It was getting closer and closer to her turn at the counter. She thought of Ruth, drunk on the plane with a hot towel over her eyes. A security guard brought a young black girl outside and made her stand in front of her duffle bag while a guard unzipped it on the pavement. The girl looked younger than Melissa. She kept her hands by her hips and anxiously curled and uncurled her fists as the dog buried its snout in her clothes. When Melissa was approaching the counter she decided to say she was staying at an Airbnb but couldn't remember the address. Let them send her back to Montreal. But the woman at the counter politely asked to see her passport and then told her she could get back on the bus.

MELISSA HAD COPIED instructions on how to get the junkyard in tiny handwriting on the inside cover of the note-
book she'd bought for the trip. As her bus pulled into the
station, she texted Ruth to let her know she'd arrived.
There was a security guard at the top of the escalator in
a navy suit and a cap with a brim.

"Grey? Blue? Blue-grey?" he asked her. "I'm trying to
figure out what colour your eyes are. You're looking for
the subway?"

Melissa showed him her tiny notes and he pointed
her in the right direction. Before descending into the
subway she checked her phone but there were still no
messages from Ruth. There was a chance her flight had
been delayed.

It was quarter after six in the morning when Melissa
walked out of the subway station into Times Square. It
wasn't completely light out. She was nervous at the ATM.

She found Central Park. She bought a coffee and sat
in the grass watching very young boys play baseball and
listening to the Brooklyn accent of the coach yelling at
them. Her back was aching from dragging her duffle bag
around; her armpits were wet with cold sweat. There
were two more hours before they could check into the
Airbnb and still no word from Ruth.

When she got to the junkyard, Ruth was drinking
a mojito in the parking lot with a group of men, artists
who used the garage as a workspace and a place to crash.

"Sorry — my phone died," Ruth said when she saw
Melissa's face. Melissa could tell she was drunk and there

was no point being mad. Ruth threw an arm around Melissa's shoulders, dragging her in close, all the guys watching them.

"I need to put my bag down and change," Melissa said.

One of the men led them across the parking lot to their trailer.

"How successful do you think those guys really are?" Melissa asked Ruth when they were alone in the camper that night, after barbecuing in the junkyard with the artists. Ruth was on the bed above her. From their tiny window they could see the flare of a blowtorch severing hunks of metal for a sculpture.

"We should google them when we find Wi-Fi."

When she woke up the next morning Ruth wasn't in the trailer.

"Ruth?" She could tell she was gone because when Ruth was in the bunk above her it sagged down several inches; the mattress was held up with a wire netting that almost touched Melissa's forehead if she lay on her back. Ruth had closed the screen door but left the inside one open. Anyone walking by could see Melissa sleeping in her tank top and underwear. She batted the door shut and put on a bra and jean shorts.

Ruth was sitting at a kitchen island in the centre of the warehouse. She and the red-haired actor from the day before were both wearing towels and Ruth's long hair was whip-straight, the way it always got when it was wet. They were hunched together over an iPhone.

'There you are!" Ruth said. As soon as she looked up

Melissa could tell she was high. "I was just telling Eric about you wondering if he was legit famous or not. He's showing me his music video, it's really great, come see."

"I never said we were a huge deal or anything," Eric said.

"I didn't mean—"

Melissa felt grateful when Ruth interrupted her. "Eric, do you have any more weed? Melissa is still all fucked up from the overnight bus, she needs weed and coffee."

Eric pushed a small tin across the table to Melissa.

"You have to get a shower, the shower is so beautiful," Ruth said.

"John built it himself, he knows plumbing and carpentry," Eric said.

They walked across the junkyard to their trailer so Ruth could get dressed. A man in the street did a long, low wolf whistle.

"You shouldn't be out here in a towel, it's dangerous, it's stupid," Melissa said.

"What are we going to do today?" Ruth asked.

"I want to walk around Chinatown."

"Eric's band is playing at a café down the street this afternoon. I kind of think we should go to that."

"What? They suck. You hate that kind of music."

"I want to make friends. You can go do your touristy stuff."

Melissa got lost in Chinatown just as it was getting dark. She had bought a puppet of a dragon made of velveteen and faux fur and covered in gems. Each of its legs and the centre of its back were tied to a wooden cross that you jerked to make it dance. She'd bought it for her brother because it was about the same size as the kittens.

She walked a long block, not sure if she was going in the right direction, holding the dragon up in the breeze. Its long paper tongue flapped out of its open jaws. It was much cooler out than when she'd left the trailer, and she wished she hadn't worn shorts. She recognized the fish market and narrow side street where she'd bought the dragon, but she couldn't remember in what order she'd encountered them. She texted Ruth. She was aware of how vulnerable and touristy she looked, wandering back and forth with the puppet and not enough clothes on.

She bought a falafel for five dollars in a small restaurant with three tables. She placed her order and the guy working the cash put four falafel balls in the microwave. She laid her cell phone on the table, waiting for Ruth to respond. She ate the falafel as slowly as possible so she wouldn't have to leave. The man at the cash watched sports on a small TV behind the counter, looking up only when people came to pick up takeout orders. The sun had completely set outside the restaurant but it wasn't a dark night.

She was searching Google Maps for the street the junkyard was on when a text came through from Ruth.

This is Eric. Ruth is having her stomach pumped at New York Methodist Hospital, Prospect Park. I'm with her, but I have to go to work.

The man at the counter wrote directions for Melissa on the cover of a takeout menu. When she got into the street, it was darker than it had seemed from inside the restaurant. She looked at the list of subway stations and street names and decided to take a cab. She stepped off the curb and lifted an arm; it was the first time she'd ever hailed a cab.

The traffic made the ride painfully slow. People on bikes were passing them. She sat in the back with the dragon stretched out on its belly in her lap like a cat, her cell phone face-up in her palm in case Eric or Ruth texted.

"That fucking idiot, I didn't need my stomach pumped." Ruth was wearing a white paper gown. She looked pale and skinny and there was an IV in her arm.

"The nurse said you did. What happened? You were passed out and they brought you here?"

"The nurse said my pulse was critically slow. I feel fine, I would have been fine. How much is this going to cost? I want to leave." Ruth pinched the IV tube.

"Don't. Jesus, get your money's worth. Look what I got my brother." She held up the dragon.

"We need to get out of here. The longer I'm here the more this will cost," Ruth said.

"Did they tell you how much it's going to be? We can probably cover it between us, right?"

"I want to get out of here."

Melissa waved a nurse into the room.

"My friend wants to be discharged."

Melissa went out front to bum a cigarette while Ruth filled out some paperwork at the front desk. After the fluorescent lighting in the hospital, it seemed even darker outside. She moved down the road a little to stand under a streetlight. Soon Ruth was walking toward her in the flimsy aqua-coloured jumper she'd been wearing that morning.

"I shouldn't have gone to that show, you were right, the music was bad." Ruth slid an arm around Melissa's waist.

"Why would you want to be friends with some lame indie rock/folk dude?" Melissa was enjoying the warmth of Ruth's arm.

"Right?" Ruth shivered.

Melissa stepped onto the curb and hailed them a cab.

That night she and Ruth slept together in the bottom bunk of the trailer. Ruth was behind Melissa with an arm around her stomach. Their legs were touching and a slick of their mixed sweat made their skin slippery. They spent the last days of the trip together. They avoided the artists from the warehouse. Eric knocked on the door of the trailer one morning when they were getting dressed and they froze. Ruth put a finger over her lips and they waited for him to walk away.

"Ken just texted me about a job in South Korea," Ruth told her on the second-last morning.

"He's taking it? How long will he be gone?"

"He said he might be able to get us in on it," Ruth said. "He's passing our headshots along."

"Holy shit. How long do you think that flight is?"

"He says he'll text us if he hears anything."

The hospital bill had eaten up all of Ruth's money, but Melissa still had three thousand dollars left. She bought them beautiful vintage dresses. They took the subway to Coney Island and got calf-deep in the dirty ocean. They googled "trendy bars in Manhattan" and wore their new dresses to them.

When Melissa got back to Montreal she dropped her bag off at the apartment and went to the Gadbois community centre pool by herself. She watched a gangly boy climb the ladder to the diving board. Outside the plateglass windows two highways looped around each other in the air, carrying a steady stream of transport trucks through blue sky. A remixed reggae song was humming from the speakers.

The boy's wet eyebrows were raised up into his high forehead. One foot then the other on the mint-ice-cream-coloured plank. Two skinny elbows jerking in time to the music, sunlight splashing all over his wet curls and the surface of the pool. Melissa decided to book a plane ticket home. The boy's skinny shoulders swinging and head bobbing all along the length of the board. Then a graceful flop into the air between beats.

Her mother came to get her at the St. John's airport at four in the morning. Melissa unzipped her suitcase on the living room floor and took out a T-shirt to wear to bed. On her way to her bedroom she pushed her brother's door open. The kittens were curled together at the bottom of his bed. They weren't really kittens anymore. Their middles had elongated but their legs were short and their heads were still tiny. She felt she'd made it home just in time.

All Set Up

ANTHONY ONCE OVERHEARD Margaret on the phone saying Rich Reid gave her the best head she ever had and now she was afraid no one as skilled as Rich would ever eat her out again. She was almost crying.

Margaret was six months pregnant at a Halloween party on Pleasant Street. Anthony walked in on her alone in the living room with Johnny Dawe. Even though there were two long couches they were sitting so close together their legs were touching. Everyone knew she was pregnant. She was dressed in grey leggings and a grey top and she had a fanny pack with a stuffed baby kangaroo sticking out of the zipper. There was a little swell to her tummy. Johnny was drunk but Anthony knew that Margaret was completely sober. Johnny was looking down her shirt and when they saw Anthony in the doorway the two of them shifted apart. There was a lamp on in the corner and black and orange streamers drooping from the ceiling. Anthony just walked away. It wasn't that he thought anything had happened, it was the way they peeled their legs apart when they saw him. Anthony turned on the threshold and wandered into the basement. He did three or four shots and got belligerent and she went home without him.

He had a blurry memory of grabbing Audrey Lévesque's butt while they were dancing in the basement after Margaret went home. Audrey was dressed as a ring-master; she was wearing shorts covered in gold sequins. When Anthony squeezed her ass the sequins had ruffled and dug into his palm.

AFTER MARGARET LEFT for the breakfast shift, Anthony took their daughter over to Fred's. Fred had a two-bed-room apartment on King's Road. One bedroom was a pen for his chinchillas. Anthony left the stroller in the front porch next to a bag of garbage and a bike wheel. He held Lee on his hip on the way up the narrow stairs to the apartment, her short legs kicking gently on either side of his torso, her fist curled against his chest. He let himself in.

Susan, a girl Fred was seeing, was eating a bowl of cereal at the kitchen table in shorts and a sports bra. He'd met her before; she looked young to him. Lately everyone his friends were seeing looked young.

"This is your daughter?" She put the cereal down and came to stand next to them. Lee pressed her face into Anthony's jacket. "Fred's in with the chinchillas, I'll get him." Susan picked up her cereal and walked to the chin-chilla room. Anthony followed. Her shorts were too big for her. There was space between the waistband and her narrow hips.

There was a baby gate in the doorway. Fred was sitting cross-legged in the middle of the chinchilla room, rolling a joint on a slim, hardcover *National Geographic* book with a Moon rover on the cover. The chinchillas were tumbling around together in the corner, chirping.

"Oh my God, look at you, Dad! Hiya, Lee." Fred stood up carefully, holding the book in front of him with two hands. He walked over slowly, making sure the little mound of weed didn't shift. He cooed at Lee from the other side of the baby gate. Fall light was pouring through the window behind him.

"Are those chinchillas mating or what?" Anthony asked.

"They're friends, you never cuddle with your friends? Here, let me out. Let's go out on the deck." Fred passed Susan the book and lifted his knees high, one at a time, to step over the baby gate into the hall.

Anthony let Susan hold Lee while he jogged back down to the front porch for the stroller. He was surprised that it made him nervous to leave his daughter alone with Fred and his girlfriend.

Anthony put Lee back in the stroller and left her inside the house, facing onto the deck so he could watch her through the screen door. Fred had an old computer monitor with an elongated back in the corner of the deck, the screen pointed at the sky. He'd smashed the glass, filled it with soil and planted a thistle in it. Susan had wrapped herself in a flannel jacket with a quilted lining and was sitting on the rail of the deck, her socked feet kicking back and forth in the air.

"And how does Mom feel about you smoking weed when you've got Lee?" Fred asked.

"Oh, Margaret doesn't care." Actually, it was a topic he and Margaret avoided. As he inhaled, things were coming sharply into focus—like the yellow that was creeping over the leaves on a branch that flopped over the rail of the deck. "Did I tell you I have a job interview?" Anthony asked.

"You told me, you told me like three times. Oh! I've been meaning to tell you, I have an idea for you, about your new job." Fred was tugging a cigarette out of a full pack. He handed one to Susan and one to Anthony.

Susan was waving at Lee through the screen door but Lee didn't notice. She was playing with a small plastic book that she'd found in a tangle of blankets in the seat of her stroller.

"Let's hear it," Anthony said.

"We went to a meet-and-greet for Susan's cousin's graduation and they basically had photo collages with music playing behind them."

Susan passed Fred the joint and he licked a finger and dragged it around the smouldering edge of the paper.

"Graduation videos?" Anthony asked. From the deck he could almost see the building where Margaret worked. "High school kids have cameras on their phones. They have a million fucking photos of themselves already."

"Funeral videos."

Susan burst out laughing. It was before noon and the day was clear and cold.

"That's very different than a wedding video," Anthony said. "I mean, how would you market it?"

"You make pamphlets, you bring them around to the funeral homes, get them to pass them out along with the ones about coffins, or even just leave them in the lobby. I think there's a market for it." Fred turned to Susan for backup and she nodded, suddenly serious.

"Right now there is," she said. "In ten years the people organizing funerals will be able to make the videos themselves, but you could cash in on it now. The spouses of people who are dying now don't know how to edit a video." Anthony noted how authoritative she could be.

"It could be your own niche in the company, get yourself promoted. Innovation, upward mobility. That kind of thing."

"I don't know that there's a lot of room for upward mobility at LoveStoryMedia." Anthony was anxious to have the joint passed his way.

"Once you start bringing in that funeral-video money there will be. I mean, you could do it tastefully is the thing." Fred ground the joint into the rail of the deck. "That was dead."

ANTHONY HAD FOUND LoveStoryMedia on Craigslist. It paid better than minimum wage. When he arrived at

Ponderosa for the interview, Lydia Ramsey handed him a glossy business card. It was brown, with the company's name surrounded by tapioca-coloured bubbles.

"Just so you know I'm not wasting your time," she said. Lydia Ramsey was old enough to be his mother. She was wearing a business suit with a rhinestone brooch on the lapel and a pair of running sneakers. They went over to the buffet and made small talk as they slid their plastic trays along the rails. Lydia Ramsey was a vegetarian. She'd just had her van in to be repaired and felt the mechanic had ripped her off. Anthony nodded a lot. He lifted a ladle of wrinkled grey peas onto his tray. They stopped at the drink station and poured fountain drinks into plastic cups. Anthony tapped the straw dispenser.

"This lunch is on the company, by the way," she said as they sat down with their food.

"Oh, thanks so much," Anthony said.

Lydia Ramsey dipped a chip in a puddle of creamed corn. "I feel good about this."

"Thanks." Anthony was sawing through a piece of breaded chicken breast. The fork felt slippery in his hand. He tried to pin the chicken down but it skidded back and forth across his plate.

Lydia Ramsey took a piece of folded-up paper out of her purse and opened it beside her tray. She'd printed his resumé out in lilac-coloured ink.

"Right. You have a film degree, that's wonderful. And you'll be able to wear those pants to the weddings. You'll need dress shoes but this is a wonderful start."

Anthony chewed a wet lump of meat. Lydia Ramsey had her back to the window and he could see cars zipping along the road behind her shoulder. She dug another chip into the sloppy little hill of corn.

"The whole process is pretty straightforward. I'll get Wendy to give you a run-through tomorrow. We'll have the Klein rushes then, so she can show you what we're looking for. The essential shots."

THERE WERE NIGHTS after Margaret went back to work that she came home sweaty and exhausted. She'd get into bed in just her underwear and curl into him. She would fling her thigh over his stomach and he would nudge her calf off his junk and rub her back.

He could drift off before she got home but he couldn't sleep deeply until she was there.

"They were so mean to me," she'd say, and press her damp forehead into him. He'd smell the grease in her hair and grab a handful of her butt.

"Want me to slit their throats?" he'd ask, rubbing up and down her back and then slipping his hand down the back of her underwear.

"Yeah." She'd clench the muscles in her leg and wiggle her stomach against his side, mashing her breasts into him.

"'Cause I'll do it. I'll wait for them to leave the restaurant and haul them into an alley."

"Do it."

"Just say the word, baby." He'd reach two fingers up into her.

"I'm saying it." Her voice would be shallow from him wiggling his fingers in her.

"As soon as you say it, it's done. You want me to wrestle them into the alley and slit their throats for you?"

"Yes, definitely."

And then he'd haul her on top of him and they'd fuck.

"Should I pull out?" he asked her sometimes. Sometimes he just pulled out but sometimes he asked. He didn't even really know if he wanted another baby. When he'd been waiting for hours and then he heard the front door open and she got in the bed and asked him to untangle an elastic matted into the back of her hair and strip her out of her skirt and nylons and rub her aching arches for a few minutes and they fucked—all of this very quietly, so they didn't wake Lee up on the other side of their bedroom wall then he wanted to have a whole slew of kids with her. Or when she came home and Lee had been crying and he'd brought her into their bed. He'd lie on his side with Lee's bum pressed into his belly and Margaret's belly pressed into his back. That made him want another kid. He imagined whispering to Lee about how her mom and new baby sister were sleeping upstairs.

Other nights they'd fight. About the state of the house. About whether the cartoon Lee was watching was too violent. About money, about which bills needed to be paid and which could wait, about whether twelve dollars was an outrageous amount to spend on a steak, about whether Margaret should keep her flip phone or upgrade. About whether she would rather be sleeping with Rich Reid.

ANTHONY PARKED NEXT to a cart corral in the lot of the Torbay Road Mall. There was a very-early-morning dampness that he had forgotten existed. Tiny beads of condensation were shining on the roof of a car that'd been in the parking lot all night. The sun slid down the hood of his car and gathered in a wide dent in the bumper from the time he'd nudged a fire hydrant while parking. Through the back window Anthony saw a heap of crumbs resting in the seam of Lee's car seat.

Anthony went in through the Dollarama entrance and passed a tanning salon and a used-clothing store. When he opened the door of LoveStoryMedia an electronic bell sounded.

There were blown-up wedding photos on the walls. The woman at the front desk was eating from a small container of yogurt. She turned her head slowly away from the screen. Suddenly her attention was focused on him. She waited for him to tell her what he wanted.

"Lydia asked me to come in this morning."

"You're here for a consultation?" She laid her spoon on the desk. He could see a streak of saliva drying on its curved back. She had a nametag saying "Wendy" pinned to her sweater. Her fingers hovered just above the keyboard. She was framed on either side of the reception desk by cream-coloured ceramic vases with bursts of plastic lilies dusted in glitter.

"No, she interviewed me. She told me to come in."

Wendy let anger play on her face for just a moment and then she reeled it back in. Anthony stood on the bristly acrylic welcome mat inside the front door, waiting for further instructions.

"She should have let me know you were coming for training. Luckily I'm doing one now. You can watch. Come around here."

He stood close to the woman's office chair. She had her legs crossed and was using the foot that was planted on the floor to make the chair sway back and forth. Standing above her he could see deep into her shirt, he could see where her bra met her sternum and a little roll of chub that the bottom of her bra rested in. She was leaning into the screen, an elbow on the computer desk, holding her bottom lip between her thumb and forefinger. Each time she swayed to the left the padded armrest bumped against his thigh.

"See them breaking the glass? For a Jewish wedding you need that, but Jeff kept screwing around with the zoom. That's an essential shot, so you just have to work with what the cameraman gives you."

She had a lazy hand resting on the mouse. She dragged the cursor and moved backward through the footage. She unbroke the glass again and again, shaving seconds off the shot.

"What're you? Catholic?" she asked. There was a mini-fridge nestled under her desk and she tugged it open.

"Nothing—I mean atheist, I guess."

"I mean what were you raised? Do you want a yogurt? They're strawberry."

"I wasn't raised anything. My mom isn't religious. We weren't religious growing up."

"I'm just trying to ask what type of weddings you've been to. Christian ones?" She bent down and took a sleeve of cookies out of the fridge.

"Yeah, Christian ones."

"Okay, well, we mostly do Christian weddings anyway, those videos will be easier. You'll just sort of instinctually know what shots you need."

WHEN ANTHONY THOUGHT about a second baby he thought about just before Lee. There had been a baby shower at one of Margaret's friend's houses. Margaret took the truck and came back with five garbage bags of clothes. Some for her and some for the baby, elastic waistbands for both of them. There was the stroller with its rusted joints, creaking and snapping when they unfolded it in the hallway. Margaret dumped the bags out on the living room floor while Anthony sat on the velveteen humpty his mother had given them. Margaret held up each piece of clothing for him before sorting it—a pile for her and a pile for the baby. A rattle fell out of a rolled-up jumper and bounced on the living room floor.

"We're going to be getting used to that sound," Margaret said.

Anthony lifted a pair of pants out of Margaret's pile and held them against his hips. He put his coffee down and took his pants off. Margaret was holding up a tiny coat by the shoulders. She didn't notice him struggling to get the cuff of his jeans off his heel. He put the maternity pants on to make her laugh. They were spandex but printed like acid-wash jeans. Margaret dropped the coat onto the baby's pile. She sat on top of the clothes and the heap spread out beneath her; she was laughing so much at the hideous pants that she started choking. He joined her on their bounty. Stained terry-cloth bibs with crinkly plastic lining. A monkey with jelly-filled hands and feet for chewing on. They cuddled and burrowed until their shoulders were against the floor and the clothes were dunes around them.

He wore the pants to bed, his ankle hair curled up over the cuff. They left the clothes on the living room floor for two weeks. Partly because they were both working and hadn't made space for them in the bedroom, but also because it was a shrine to what was to come.

There was also anxiety about money then. Vivid dreams about empty houses and menacing letters. After those dreams he would lie awake, sweating, with a roll of comforter between his thighs. There was no undoing what they'd done. The weight of not knowing what they'd taken on. Also, the thought of the actual birth disgusted him — he had to keep his face from contorting at the sound of the word.

One night Margaret got in the bath and he made them

peanut butter and chocolate milkshakes in the food pro-
cessor. They drank them out of beer steins, him sitting
on the toilet with his jeans rolled up to the knee and his
bare feet submerged in her bath.

"This is giving me an ice cream headache." The steam
made her hair curly. Her breasts were huge and her belly
was like an upside-down mixing bowl; the water made
her tight skin glimmer.

"That's how you know you're alive," he told her.

"I wasn't feeling confused about being alive." She
kicked warm water at him, soaking his T-shirt and the
crotch of his jeans.

He wanted Lee to experience the pre-baby giddiness.
He and Margaret clinging to each other everywhere they
went, two sets of hands on the steering bar of the shopping cart at the supermarket.

EVEN THOUGH LOVESTORYMEDIA was in a small space,
Anthony had an office. There was a window that looked
out at the parking lot. He had never had an office before. He bought a springy young spider plant at the
supermarket.

"I just sent you the rushes from the weddings we did
this weekend. We'll go over them together, okay? Just get
your email open there." Wendy was dragging her wheelie
chair over the carpet into his office. She bent her knees
and tugged on the arm to get the chair to bounce over
the threshold. When she stood back up her skirt was all

bunched up; a centimetre higher and he would have been able to see her ass in her tights.

He had a photo of the day they brought Lee home propped against the bottom of his monitor. Margaret was sitting on the couch in her winter coat and Lee was in her car seat on the sofa next to her.

"Okay, here's a list of shots we always grab at Christian weddings." She held up a wrinkled printout. "I've checked their file and they don't want any extra stuff; a straight-forward video like this is going to be about twenty to forty minutes. We're gonna start with the bride walking down the aisle. You just drag the clips you want into this file here."

He opened the video and an electric organ played out of the speakers on his desk.

"Okay, actually I like to start with the empty aisle, that's just my style, opening shot of the church. Tom usually does a scan of the crowd. Just select it like this. You don't have to watch the whole video, you can skim through a lot of it." She'd pulled her chair up to his. Her arm grazed his chest when she used the mouse. She didn't say anything about the photo of Margaret and Lee. Her arm moved up and down over his nipples and they got hard and he didn't think there was any way she hadn't noticed. He let his knee flop out and rest against her thigh.

MARGARET'S FAMILY WERE hippies; there was a photo of her naked mother in the bathroom of her parents' house.

Also, Margaret was never scolded for wearing mismatched socks. Anthony secretly believed this was why Margaret was such a flirt. Why she let vegetables wilt in the back of the fridge and left her clothes on the floor in every room of the house.

Anthony lay three chicken breasts slathered in barbecue sauce on the grill. There was the nub of an old joint in the front pocket of his shirt. He'd brought Lee's high chair out onto the deck with him. It was getting to be time to switch to a booster seat; the tray of the high chair dug into her belly. He pinched the roach to his lips. When the chicken was done he dropped the roach between the boards of the deck and carried Lee inside.

When Anthony was a little high, his favourite thing to do was clean. He put Lee in her playpen out in the hallway and washed the floor of the kitchen. Lee dangled a stuffed unicorn out of the playpen by a thick ankle and dropped it. He left the patio door open even though it was cold, and the smell of barbecue filled the apartment. He passed the toy back to Lee again and again. He squashed the mop against the bottom of the stove, spraying the cupboards with frothy floor cleaner. He smeared suds back and forth over the dried liquid beneath the fridge door. He thought maybe the fumes from the cleaner were bad for Lee's mushy little undeveloped brain so he pushed the playpen further down the hallway.

When Margaret got home from work she was starving. She ran upstairs to change and he brought the high chair in from the back deck to get ready for dinner.

"This is a feast," Margaret said when they were all settled in the tidy kitchen. He nodded, moving some cut-up pieces of potato from his plate onto Lee's tray.

"Are you high?" she asked.

"No."

"You are." Margaret put down her utensils.

"I actually put a lot of work into this meal. Can we just have a nice dinner together?" He sounded pissier than he'd meant to.

"I guess not." Margaret picked up her plate and stomped upstairs.

"Come on, let's start over." He stood in the hallway calling up to the second floor. He heard Margaret turn the bath on.

Anthony cleared the table and did the dishes and Margaret still hadn't come out of the bathroom. He glanced at his phone and saw that Fred had invited him over.

"We don't have to sit around here waiting for Mommy to get over her little hissy fit," Anthony whispered to Lee as he bundled her into her coat, coaxing her arms through the puffy sleeves.

"I'm taking Lee over to Fred's," he called. He heard the slosh of her sitting up in the tub.

When he got there Lee had fallen asleep in the stroller. He realized he hadn't even texted Fred back to let him know he was coming. He probably should have said he was bringing Lee. Fred might be having a bunch of people over for a party. The deep tiredness of having smoked weed in the daytime was settling into his muscles and the thought of making conversation with people, maybe people he didn't know, seemed impossible. He turned the stroller around.

Margaret was asleep in a T-shirt when he got back; her hair had made the pillows wet. He curled himself around her and put his cold fingers on her hot belly.

"I love you. I got that job, I cleaned the kitchen," he said, with his cheek on the damp pillow. She was asleep but he could tell he'd been forgiven.

ANTHONY ALWAYS ANSWERED the phone when Margaret called. No matter where he was or who he was with.

"I think I want to get a turtle," Margaret said. Anthony pictured her pacing back and forth in the kitchen with Lee on her hip.

"Okay."

"You like the idea? I've wanted a turtle ever since I was a little girl. I mean, on and off."

"I used to want a lizard. When I was a teenager I wanted a really big one, like the kind that rides on your shoulder." Anthony had stopped at the lights three inter-sections from his co-worker's house.

"Really? We could have plants growing in the tank."

"Sure. Listen, I'm in bad traffic." What he didn't want was to be parked in Wendy's driveway talking to Margaret.

"Okay, I don't have to work until the five tomorrow, we could go in the afternoom, what do you think?"

"Okay. But I've really got to let you go now." The third intersection was a yellow light and he slowed where he normally would have glided through.

"Okay, I'm excited about this. I love you."

"Love you too." Anthony pulled into a parking lot down the street from Wendy's house. It was an older Shoppers Drug Mart, destined to be torn down soon. There was a dark section in the middle of the backlit sign and part of the parking lot was roped off with security tape. He laid some DVDs from work under the seat and locked the doors. He walked quickly down the block and rang Wendy's doorbell.

She was wearing a cream-coloured silk housecoat when he arrived and she kissed him. Her bare feet in the grime from other people's wet shoes.

"My roommates are gone out." She had noticed him taking in the sneakers and high-heeled boots that were tossed around in the porch. The house smelled like spaghetti sauce and there was a tinge of orange around her mouth but she tasted like toothpaste. "Let's go up to my room."

Anthony bent over and undid his laces. She waited on the steps while he took off his boots.

Her bedroom was almost empty. The gold-painted feet of a lamp rested on an overturned milk crate next to a mattress on the floor. There were three overflowing hampers pushed up against the wall. Several reusable supermarket bags filled with stacks of books took up the centre of the room, their stiff handles sticking straight up.

"I don't have it all set up yet, I need my brother to help me bring over my furniture."

"You've got a nice big window," he told her. She was working on a Ph.D. so she couldn't possibly be as young as the surroundings suggested, he thought.

She kneeled on the bed and opened her housecoat. She had on a bra made of some kind of mesh, and electric pink underwear. He sat behind her on the bed and ran a finger down her spine before undoing the hooks of her bra.

"Can you turn up the heat? The dial is right there," she said. "And shut the door, I don't think anyone will come home but just in case."

He began taking her underwear off with his teeth but in the end it involved both his hands and some hip-lifting and twisting on her part. When he dropped the underwear on the floor he noticed an almost-dried-out tea bag in a mug that was nestled up against the mattress.

THEY PICKED UP Lee from preschool on the way to the pet store. The preschool was in a church basement. Margaret waited in the truck while Anthony went down the cool stone steps to the playroom. It was a drizzly morning.

In the stairway he thought about Wendy's nubbly sheets. Her breasts were very different from Margaret's. He had sort of forgotten how different breasts could feel, the variations in shape and firmness.

The children were crowded around a plastic castle with a set of stairs and a short slide. There was a skinny teenage girl in khaki shorts and a baggy T-shirt sitting cross-legged on the small platform between the stairs and the slide. She was stamping each child's hand at the mouth of the slide. He didn't see Lee at first. She was picking at a pile of Lego blocks, undistracted by the bustle around the castle.

Lee led him to her cubby and he helped her wriggle into her rain jacket. He used a pen tied to the attendance book with a piece of yellow yarn to sign Lee out.

"It's raining out there." He tugged her hood up.

They climbed up out of the playroom and made their way across the wet pavement to where Margaret was waiting for them.

In the truck Margaret showed Lee a video on her phone of a baby turtle eating a raspberry. Its beak was able to nip only a tiny bit of the berry at a time. It slowly made a dent in the centre of the berry. It stuck its neck out further and further to get at the fruit instead of wad-dling up to it.

Lee leaned her head against the sleeve of her mother's rain jacket, quietly watching the video.

They went to a pet store in Foxtrap that Margaret's cousin owned. A very old man stood at the cash. His bottom lip rested limply on his gums and his jaw was working in a jerky circle. His hands were in the pockets of a fleece vest. Anthony approached the counter. Before he could speak a much younger man — really, a boy — darted out of an office in the back and got between him and the old man.

"We're looking for a turtle," Anthony said. The store was warm and moist and filled with the burbling of many fish tanks.

"Gord's my cousin," Margaret added. "I'm Marg."

"Baby turtle?" asked the boy.

Anthony looked at Margaret, who was holding Lee's hand.

"Sure," Margaret answered.

"Okay, right this way." The boy led them through a dim corridor of fish tanks stacked on metal shelving. Anthony paused in front of a pink-tailed catfish curling and uncurling itself, opening its human lips for him. Lee tugged on the leg of his pants.

The baby turtles were in the back. There were about five of them crowded onto a small rock, standing on each other's backs. The price was scribbled in permanent marker on the glass of the tank: "$79.99." Lee pressed her face right up to the glass of the case. The boy was holding a small net and a temporary tank the size of a child's lunchbox with a plastic lotus flower floating in it. Neither Anthony nor Margaret said anything about the price.

"Which one should we get, Lee?" Margaret asked.

The glass tank was shockingly expensive. The food was expensive. The plastic plants that suctioned to the bottom of the tank were twenty dollars each. You had to buy an enormous bag of stones to line the tank. Still they didn't talk about how much it cost.

"How long do these guys live?" Margaret asked as she slid her card out of the bottom of the machine.

The old man rested both hands on the counter while the boy told them how often to clean the tank and feed the turtle.

Anthony carried Lee into the house, holding her against him with one arm with the temporary turtle tank in his opposite hand. Margaret took the bag of tank liner, the heavy bulk of it resting against her chest. Anthony put Lee in her playpen so he and Margaret could carry the huge glass tank in from the truck.

The little family assembled around the aquarium. Margaret poured water into the tank from a jug they used for mixing up frozen juice. It took lots of trips back and forth between the kitchen and living room.

Once the tank was full Anthony placed a dinner plate upside down on the reflective bottom of the tank. He poured the pink and purple stones down on top of it so that they would distribute evenly, a trick the boy at the pet store had described to them, and they marvelled at the way the stones glided down the sloped rim of the plate and into the corners of the tank. After Anthony took the plate out he lifted Lee up and she reached in up to her armpit to smooth stones into the empty space it had left. Finally, they lowered in the plastic castle so the turtle could spend some time sunning itself under the UV light in the lid of the tank. It was a glittery, baby blue castle with an angled turret that would allow the turtle to haul itself up out of the water.

Lee sat on the floor below the tank, staring into the world the three of them had created.

Later, when Anthony came back from tucking Lee in, he found Margaret leaning over the tank.

"I'm so glad we made this happen," she told him.

"Do you think he'll miss the other turtles?" Anthony asked. "There's not a lot going on in there."

"He can watch us."

The turtle stared out at them from its turret above the fresh new sea.

IT WAS RARE for Lydia Ramsey to be in the office. She was usually out meeting with clients in their homes, asking them what they wanted the focus of their video to be. She had explained to Anthony that some people wanted a video that strictly documented the wedding ritual and some people had a whole slew of other expectations — the bridesmaids getting dressed, the groom nervously smoking outside the hall, an interview with the flower girl.

"This is a business that flourishes through word of mouth. We have to go the extra mile, make an impression, be thought of as friends," she told Anthony as she shuffled through a pile of labelled flash drives with customers' videos on them.

"Have you ever thought about doing funeral videos?" Anthony asked.

"Is that something people are doing?"

"I don't think so, not yet."

"I think that could have a negative impact on

LoveStory's image." Lydia dropped a flash drive into her bag and snapped it shut.

"I think there's a market for it," Anthony said. "Think of how people fawn over the photo boards at a wake—it's a way of remembering communally. And we could do interviews, include home videos, it would be tasteful." His voice had gotten louder than he meant it to.

"You know what? I like hearing your ideas," Lydia said. "I like that you're thinking outside the box. But I don't think that particular idea is for us."

Anthony noticed that Wendy had been standing in the doorway, listening to the interaction. She moved out of the way to let Lydia pass.

"Back to the drawing board, I guess," Wendy said after they heard the door close behind Lydia.

ANTHONY READ THAT turtles liked to chase small fish; it was good for them, they were hunters. He took Lee to Walmart and bought a bag of tiny, glinting fish, partly just as a way to fill up a Sunday. He pushed her up and down an aisle on a children's toy that was meant to look like a ride-on lawn mower. He put her in the front of a shopping cart and wandered through popcorn makers and irons and tried to think what he would get people for Christmas. Older women stopped them and touched Lee's hair and talked to her about her dress and her little pink boots. Anthony was glad that they were out being a part of the world.

He held the knot that kept the fish baggie shut in his fist as they crossed the parking lot. In the truck he put the baggie in a compartment between the seats meant for tapes. He cringed, imagining the bag bursting, as he gently laid it on the slotted bottom of the compartment. Lee was in the back seat with a sticky handful of Smarties they'd gotten from the candy dispenser near the exit.

At home he undid the slippery knot and emptied the fish into the turtle's tank. Lee stood on a chair beside him at the sink as he scrubbed the slime off the castle with rubber gloves on. He put the turtle in the small tank they'd brought it home in while he did it. He was afraid the turtle would drown in the larger tank if it wasn't able to climb up onto the castle.

Anthony picked the scrubber and gloves off the floor by the tank and threw them in the garbage.

"Why?" Lee asked.

"Because turtle poo is very dangerous to humans. We can't get it on our dishes."

When he lowered the turtle back into the tank it moved like something that was recovering from being turned to stone. As though moving was new to it. The turtle's tiny beak was fierce and when it closed on a fish's spine it snapped it.

ANTHONY RODE IN the back of the LoveStoryMedia van with the equipment. The cameraman was driving. Lydia talked to him from the front seat.

"Today you're a roadie. You carry stuff, do anything Tom might want you to. Don't lean against the door, I hope you're not leaning against the door."

Anthony tried to edge away from the door, but they rounded a corner and he slammed against it. The door flew open and for a moment he was halfway out of the van. A slur of blue sky streamed above him. The guy behind them leaned on his horn. Somehow, by wrenching his stomach muscles, he was able to pull himself back into the van. For a moment he lay on his stomach, his cheek pressed against the plastic rivulets in the floor, the road rushing past beneath the van. Then the door swung shut.

The Landlord

THERE WERE ALWAYS ripped-open sugar packets and smears of ketchup to be wiped up. They got wiped up with the same rags that were used to wipe crusted molasses off the top of the squeeze bottles they passed out with toutons. After using the rags Mary sometimes noticed a smell on her hands that reminded her of the way her belly-button piercing smelled when it got infected. At the end of the evening shift she flipped all the chairs so their seats rested on the tables and mopped up to hits from the eighties. They always played Coast 101 at Family Restaurant.

She hated being disliked. When the dishwasher invited her into the corner of the dish pit that couldn't be seen on the security tape to do a shot of Jameson, Mary didn't feel like drinking but she did it to be likeable. To prove her likeability. She went to sweep out the bathrooms and noticed her bangs were greasy and clumping together. When she got back she did three more shots and started feeling very likeable. A customer saw her pick an onion ring off his appetizer combo and eat it while the cook was arranging the cheesy fingers on the opposite side of the plate. She found herself making eye contact as she crumbled the rest of the onion ring into her mouth. There were breadcrumbs on the front of her shirt. She wiped them off with greasy fingers.

"Go with it, take it," the cook was saying with urgency. Mary saw the customer lean in and tell his girlfriend about her eating the onion ring. She brought the plate to the table anyway.

"Can I get you anything else? A refill on your Coke?" She pretended she hadn't seen him seeing her, hoping he would begin to doubt it had happened, hoping there wouldn't be a TripAdvisor review.

He didn't tip. But he also didn't say anything after the meal, when she stood at his table while they waited together for his payment to go through.

She unravelled the twin scrolls from the debit machine and computer to do off the cash at the end of the night. The numbers were too small and blurry to manage. She would be in the next morning, so she sealed and dated the envelope with a blank cash sheet inside.

After the shift the head cook went home to his family, but the dishwasher and the line cook wanted to keep drinking. They invited her to come out with them. They waited while she locked the door, lighting cigarettes, zipping their jackets. It was mild but raining. She was starving and dizzily drunk.

Mary noticed the man as soon as they got to the bar, but at first she couldn't place him. Her co-workers slid into a booth and she sat on the dishwasher's side. He ordered them beers and she used cash from her tips to pay for them, plus a plate of nachos for the table. You could hear the rain against the windows even over the radio.

"We thought you were too normal at first but I'm starting to think you're a weirdo like the rest of us," the line cook told her.

The dishwasher ordered them a round of shots. A waitress brought them over on a brown plastic tray and laid the shot glasses on the edge of the table one by one. After they finished the shots, the dishwasher filled the small glasses with a flask he had in his pocket.

The dishwasher was a couple of years younger than she was. His chef's coat was too small; his wide wrists always stuck out below the sleeves. Now he was wearing a T-shirt with a skateboarding logo on the front. His book bag was on the floor, under the table. He unzipped the front pouch and showed them a brick of tinfoil.

"That's really good hash, my buddy hooked me up," he said, leaning across the table toward the line cook.

"Nice," the line cook said, tapping his shot glass on the table for the dishwasher to refill.

MARY HAD AN aunt who'd gone skydiving on vacation in the south of France. As the helicopter blades beat the air above a field, the instructor pointed out a small iron shed to the left of the helicopter and told them not to look at it. One woman became fixated on the shed, her aunt said, and her inability to look away drew her to it when she jumped. A sheet of the iron grazed her leg and sliced her thigh apart, exposing the bone. That was what was happening to Mary with the man at the bar.

On the way back from the bathroom, where she'd been tousling her bangs trying to make them look less greasy, she made eye contact with the man and realized he was her landlord. Now eye contact was propelling her toward the landlord against her will.

"You're the girl from Patrick Street." He was sitting with another man.

"Mary." She put out her hand. It had only been a little over a month since they'd met up to sign the lease, but it had taken her a while to remember him too.

"Can I get you a drink? Rum and Coke?" He held up his own glass. "Let me get you a rum and Coke."

"Greg, I've got to get on the go," the landlord's friend said as the landlord beckoned to the bartender.

"She's a tenant of mine, on Patrick Street."

"I'd say you're expected home soon," the landlord's friend said. He stood up and lifted his coat off the back of his chair.

Mary sat next to the landlord in the seat warmed by his friend. It wasn't until she sat down that she remembered her rent was overdue; she didn't have her half together. She saw the nachos arrive at her table, a sheet of tan wax paper sitting between the plate and chips.

"You're a student?" He was younger than her father, definitely.

"Yeah." She saw her co-workers look around for her before they started in on the nachos.

"At MUN? What're you studying?" He was wearing a golf shirt. The top button was undone and she could see his chest hair. She saw that there was also thick hair on his forearms—it was sexy to her.

"My major is in Religious Studies. You're a landlord, I mean you manage properties?" She swivelled the seat. He wasn't going to bring up the money. He probably hadn't even realized they were late with it, yet.

"I've got a few properties around. One on Byron, one on Baltimore, one right across from Brother Rice, and Patrick Street. My wife is a real estate agent."

There was a long pause. "It's really raining out there now." One of her waitressing lines.

"I'm just leaving, why don't I drop you off? I've only had one drink."

"Let me just tell my friends I'm leaving." Her polyester work pants were soaked from the walk over. They were stuck to her skin in an uncomfortable way.

When she got to the table she picked a chip off the plate.

"Who's that?" asked the line cook.

"My landlord."

"You're leaving with your landlord?" the dishwasher asked.

"I just ran into him, he offered me a ride."

"Be careful," the line cook said.

"He's just giving me a ride." She was ripping chips off the wax paper and stacking them on her palm, to eat in the car.

"I'd say you're going to end up giving him a ride," the line cook said. "He looks sleazy as fuck."

"Whatever, let her go, she's a big girl." The dishwasher finished his beer. "Let's go downtown."

In the car she felt drunker. She hadn't eaten since three o'clock. She ate her little pile of chips. There were chunks of pale tomato anchored in the cold cheese. He had K-Rock on; it was warm in the car and she felt nauseous. When they pulled up outside her house he put his hand on her thigh.

"Still having trouble with the dryer?"

"Yeah, it takes two or three cycles to get anything to dry."

"Give me a call tomorrow and remind me, I'll send someone to look at it."

"Thanks for the ride." She summoned co-ordination.

On the way to the front door the ground swooped beneath her. She lurched to the left of the door and steadied herself on the slick plastic siding. It was raining so heavily that water dripped off her nose and chin. Her keys were not in either of her coat pockets. He was idling, waiting for her to get inside. She rang the doorbell before she started going through the zippered compartment in the front of her book bag. She rang the doorbell a second time, three quick rings in a row. She glanced behind her and saw he was leaning over to unroll the passenger-side window. A bobby pin in the bag's front pouch stuck into the tender place underneath her nail and she drew her hand out and put her finger in her mouth.

"Do you want me to take you somewhere else?" he called out the window.

"No, I'm going to text my roommate, she's probably studying."

Mary listened for footsteps inside the house but there were none. She shifted things in the front pouch and felt the key. She held it up for him to see and he nodded but didn't drive away. She dropped her book bag onto the wet front step. She shimmed the key into the keyhole but it wouldn't move in the slot. She wrenched it right and left but it wouldn't move.

"I can't get the key to turn," she said from the step.

He turned off the car and got out into the rain. He took the key from her and as he turned it he rammed the door with his shoulder. It flew open and he stumbled inside.

"I'll have to do something about that, it shouldn't be sticking like that," he said as she entered the dark porch. "Maybe while I'm here I'll have a look at the dryer really quickly. If it's what I think it is, I'll let Ryan know the part he needs and save him a trip."

He drew back the curtain that separated the washer and dryer from the rest of the porch. Mary followed him in and flicked the light.

"This will only take a second." He was jerking the dryer back and forth to get it away from the wall. Then he leaned over the top of the machine to look behind it.

"Okay, see the tear in that silver tube?" he asked.

She hoisted herself up to see. The edge of the dryer dug into her stomach and acidic liquid sloshed up her throat. There were huge swaths of dryer lint on the floor.

"See the tear there? That's your problem." Their hips were touching. She became aware of his hand on her ass.

"So that's very easy to fix." When she didn't respond he squeezed her ass. She stayed leaning into the dryer and he moved behind her and pressed his hard-on into her wet slacks. He slid his hand under her coat and T-shirt, reaching from behind and holding her against him. Her hand clenched around his wrist to stop his hand from moving down her body. He had her pinned against the dryer with his pudgy stomach.

"I'm going to bed now." She made her body stiff.

He stepped away from her.

"Okay. I'll let myself out, you get yourself some water." She waited in the laundry room for him to leave.

When she heard the door close she went into the porch and locked the deadbolt.

HER GUT WAS cramping from the liquor when she woke up. She'd barely eaten the day before. She remembered that she had left the cash sheet blank and that she'd smoked two of the dishwasher's cigarettes on the way to the bar even though she barely ever smoked. She was still wearing her work clothes. The taste of cigarettes in her mouth reminded her of biting into mouldy bread. She'd wasted at least thirty-five bucks at the bar. She remembered those things before she remembered being in the laundry room with the landlord.

When she peeled her pants off, the tops of her thighs were red and covered in small pimples from the clammy polyester. She wore tights and a skirt to work. She threw up on the sidewalk on the way, yellowish liquid and soggy chips that caught in her throat and made her cough. The sky was clear blue; the spring light was rimming all the hard edges in gold. The earth was soaked and cold and ready for life to work its way up out of it.

The line cook was doing prep in the kitchen. She turned the key in the cash register with her other hand against the drawer to stop it from making a noise when it sprang open. She didn't want to draw attention to the fact that she'd messed up the settlement the night before. She took the envelope with the blank cash sheet from under the tray with the float. Fleetwood Mac was playing on the radio in the kitchen and the line cook sang along emphatically with the chorus, fading into a mumbling hum during the verse. She ripped open the top of the envelope and tossed it into the garbage. The light coming through the wide window in the front of the diner stung her brain. She uncurled the reams of paper from the debit machine and computer. The dishwasher came up the back stairs with the smell of cigarettes on him.

"How's it going?" she asked as he passed.

"Same shit different day." He didn't slow down on his way into the kitchen.

She bent over the counter, jotting the totals onto the slip as quickly as possible. It was all adding up perfectly.

When the front door opened she straightened, ready to say, "I'm sorry, we don't open for another twenty minutes," but it was Ted, the owner. He had a cardboard box of lettuce and tomatoes. His teenaged son was behind him with two bags of potatoes in each fist.

"Mary? You're in this morning?"

"Yes."

"Can you grab Len, to take this stuff?"

"Of course."

When she turned around to call out to the dishwasher, the owner laid the box on the counter.

"What's this?"

"The cash-out from last night, I'm just finishing it up."

"Why wasn't it finished last night?"

The dishwasher came out of the kitchen and lifted the box off the counter. He stood for a moment taking in the conversation. The owner's son laid the potatoes on the floor.

"I forgot about it. I'll have it done in a moment though."

"That's not the point." He picked up the torn envelope with the date in her handwriting. "You do the cash-out when it's meant to be done. This is the time for prepping for breakfast, you need to get the syrups on the tables. Len, let's move, there's more in the trunk."

After lunch service Mary changed the garbages. She lifted a sneaker over the garbage bucket and brought it down into the food scraps and coffee filters.

She was still raw from the alcohol and from getting reamed out by the owner.

"Do you think there's rats down there?" Mary stood at the top of the stairs leading to the garbage alley.

"I know there's rats down there. Ted's in a foul fucking mood because of you, and I have to deal with him." The line cook undid his bandana and put it in his back pocket.

"You saw one?"

"I saw more than one. When I'm down there having a smoke they come out and stare at me."

"You're trying to freak me out."

"I don't really care if you believe me." He took off down the stairs without offering to take the garbage down for her. He normally took the garbage down. Even lifting it out of the bucket was a struggle for her. The bag was wider than her and came up to her waist. It was probably sixty percent wet coffee grounds.

She was always pissing people off by accident in this job. Or they were pissed off already and she provoked them by not knowing where things went or which lights to turn off at the end of the night or that the French onion soup didn't come with a side of toast.

At the bottom of the stairs she propped the door to the alley open with her hip, two hands wrapped around the knot in the top of the garbage bag.

The line cook was having his smoke. "You got coffee grounds everywhere," he said.

The bottom of the bag was torn and there was putrid

garbage juice smeared across the space between the bottom of the stairs and the door.

"I didn't mean that I didn't believe you, I'm just scared of rats."

"You can't drag the bag. You better mop that up before someone slips."

There was a clumpy trail of coffee grounds going up the stairs.

MARY CLEANED DARREN Holloway's apartment twice a week for a hundred bucks. Darren Holloway's deceased wife was a friend of Mary's great aunt. His daughter lived in Alberta and emailed Mary the money.

Mr. Holloway lived up behind the Delta, close to Flower Hill Grocery. He was bald and tiny. Often when Mary rang the doorbell he didn't recognize her. She would be on the other side of the screen door and he would stare at her before pulling it open. She came on Fridays after her Women in Eastern Religions class and on Wednesdays after her Spanish Conversation class.

"Hi Mr. Holloway, I'm here to help clean up and make some lunch," she'd say when he opened the door.

Mary did the dishes first. She started by stacking them up across the length of the counter. Half a week's worth of dishes: glasses in front, closest to the sink; then mugs, plates, and bowls; and finally the crusty pots. She worked from least greasy to most greasy to get the most out of the dishwater.

"The cleaning has been a little overwhelming," he usually said as he let her in.

There was an armchair in the kitchen and he would sit behind her. Once the dishes were stacked in the dish rack she made his lunch — usually pasta with tomato sauce from a can with orange cheese grated on top of it. Someone else bought the groceries.

She set a place for him, laying a paper napkin next to his knife and fork and filling a glass with milk. She sat at the opposite side of the dining room table as he struggled to wrap the spaghetti around a shaking fork. Usually by lunch he had begun to warm up and talk to her.

He told her about different jobs he'd had. He loved telling her about the six years he operated a metal detector in a Hershey factory in New Brunswick. He'd scanned the boxes of misshapen Hershey Kisses; all the deformed chocolates were boxed up separately and sold in bulk for cheap. He'd only ever found bits of foil. Minuscule flecks. They still had to be removed, no matter how minuscule. He told her the guy who used to work Tuesdays and Thursdays had been doing it for decades and had found screws in the chocolate and, once, a filling.

"'How'd you know it was a filling?' I asked him," Mr. Holloway said. "He was terrible at paperwork. It took him two shifts to do what I could get done in an afternoon. He had the place backlogged. You couldn't read his handwriting. Who knows — you can't really trust a guy like that, a guy with no work ethic."

"Did the factory smell like chocolate?"

"Yes—not as strong as you'd think, but it was always there and you never got sick of it."

When she got back to the apartment, Brittany was studying on the sofa in the living room. Brittany was often in the living room all day, reading and making notes with the TV going. She'd hook her laptop up to the TV and play episode after episode of *The X-Files*. She kept her little weed case on the arm of the sofa. She would wrap herself in a quilt. Each time she moved, bottles of nail polish would tumble out of the blanket and thwack against the floor.

Mary couldn't concentrate on studying for more than an hour at a time. She needed silence and she needed to be sober and she needed her room to be clean. But she would come out and sit with a book open in her lap as Brittany copied dates and definitions onto loose-leaf.

"I got the landlord to check out that problem with the dryer," Mary said. "He's going to send someone to look at it." She closed her textbook.

"Great—oh, did you give him the rent money?" Brittany was writing something on a cue card.

Brittany had never met the landlord. The girls had looked at the apartment together, but Mary had signed the lease by herself—Brittany had been in class—so communicating with him had fallen into the half of the chores Mary was responsible for.

"He's going to collect it in a few days," Mary lied. "He said he'll call before he comes by." She got up and tossed her book on the couch. "I'm going to make stir fry, want some?"

She had less than twenty bucks in her bank account.

THE SHIFT AFTER the incident with the cash sheet, Mary checked the schedule taped to the cinder-block wall of the break room and saw that her name only appeared once.

"I guess Ted was pretty pissed about the cash-out thing the other day." The dishwasher had walked in and caught her staring at the schedule.

She took her black non-slip sneakers out of her book bag. She could feel that she was blushing.

"Linda is going to be out next week—her son's getting surgery on his jaw. They've got to fly to the mainland for it. She might have asked for extra this week to make up for it." The dishwasher was backtracking, trying to save them both from her embarrassment.

The line cook was chopping onions in the adjacent prep room and the break room was full of the raw smell.

"And you have another job anyway, right?" the dishwasher asked her.

"It's not a big deal. I don't care." She took an elastic out of her coat pocket and pulled her hair into a ponytail; she cried easily from onions and she wanted to get out of there.

"I just came in here to get my smokes." The dishwasher held up his cigarettes and jogged down the steps to the garbage alley.

MARY WOKE UP late and decided not to go to Women in Eastern Religions. She walked to the corner store in the leggings and sweatshirt she'd worn to bed and bought a carton of chocolate milk. The air was warm; a fine mist was darkening the pavement.

The landlord had left her a voicemail message; she deleted it without listening to it. She'd gotten paid from Family Restaurant but she still had less than half of her half of the rent in the bank. She would get money from Darren Holloway's daughter in a week, but that would only be enough if she didn't spend any of it and there was hardly anything to eat at the house.

Her mother had told her she wouldn't lend her any more money unless she graduated. Mary only needed six more credits to finish her degree, but she always dropped courses. She'd sleep in and miss a class and then when she went back she was disoriented. She hated floundering for an answer in front of the class. And if she got a bad grade on an assignment, she couldn't face going back to the classroom knowing that the prof thought she was stupid — that everyone in the room had been judged and she'd been found to be in the bottom tier. She hated going to school in the first place because she would run into profs whose classes she had stopped going to in previous semesters.

To punish herself for not going, she spent the morning flipping through Facebook photos of people she'd gone to high school with who had nice, well-paying jobs. She sat on her bed in the saggy, slept-in leggings, drinking milk from the carton. She could hear Brittany in the kitchen making stovetop espresso and blending a smoothie. She waited quietly in her room for Brittany to go to class because she didn't feel like talking to her. That meant she was late leaving for Mr. Holloway's.

Halfway there the mist gathered itself into fat raindrops. At first there were long intervals and wide spaces between the drops, but soon they multiplied and picked up momentum. When Mr. Holloway looked at her through the screen door, she was soaked.

"Hi, Mr. Holloway, I'm here to do some cleaning for you."

"You're drenched." Mr. Holloway let her in and went to his bedroom.

She began sorting the dishes in the kitchen. Her wet socks left imprints of her feet all over the linoleum.

"Put this on and throw your clothes in the dryer." Mr. Holloway laid a pile of folded clothes on the table.

Mary changed in the bathroom. She looked at herself in the skinny full-length mirror screwed to the back of the door. She was wearing custard yellow shorts that came down past her knees and a polyester blouse with lace on the collar. A summer outfit belonging to the late Mrs. Holloway. It smelled like baby powder.

Mary emptied her purse on the top of the dryer and put it in with her clothes. She peeled her socks off and threw them in too.

"Much better," Mr. Holloway called from the living room couch when she came out of the laundry room in the dry clothes.

She scrubbed out a pot with crusted-on oatmeal in her bare feet and billowy outfit. There was a branch pressed against the small window above the sink. She saw a bright green bud untwist itself into a leaf in the rain.

MARY WAS PLANNING to clean the kitchen so it would be tidy when Brittany got off work. She took a dishtowel from the drawer and noticed a couple of ketchup packets in the front of the drawer. Then she saw they were husks of ketchup packets. They'd been torn open and cleaned out. She could see teeth had ripped them and she thought the word "mice" just as she noticed the tail. There was a rat curled in the back. Its tail was as long as the inside of the drawer and thicker than a pencil. It didn't move. It didn't have a pointy face; it had a flat, chinchilla-like face and it was looking at her. She took her phone out of her pocket and called the landlord.

"Hi — it's Mary, from Patrick Street. There's a rat in my kitchen."

"Are you sure it's not a mouse?"

"I'm looking at it right now: its body is as big as my sneaker. It's just sitting there."

"Is there any way you can trap it? I'll come right now, I'm just around the corner."

He normally sent a repair guy, Ryan. Mary was afraid to look away from the drawer. If the rat moved she wanted to know where it went. She turned around to get the broom and when she looked back the rat was in the front of the drawer, sitting on its hind legs.

The doorbell rang and she had to leave the rat to let the landlord in. He untied his shoes and left them on the mat in the porch, even though Mary had opened the door in sneakers with jagged salt stains across the toes. When they got to the kitchen, the rat was gone. Mary saw the landlord noticing the pile of dirty dishes next to the sink. She was still holding the broom.

He took off his jacket and hung it on the back of a chair.

"This is the drawer here?"

"See the ketchup packets? I didn't notice any signs of rats—I've had mice before, I know what to look for, and nothing was chewed up, rice or crackers or anything like that, I haven't seen any shit around. Those packets were the first thing I saw."

The landlord opened the cupboard below the drawer.

"There's a small flashlight in the pocket of my jacket, can you grab it for me? We'll try and find the hole and stuff it. I've got poison in the car—we'll put that in the hole and then seal it up. Do you have any steel wool?" The landlord was speaking from inside the cupboard, just his ass in light denim outside the cabinet. He was like the witch from "Hansel and Gretel," half in the oven. Mary reached in one pocket and found the flashlight. The second pocket had his wallet, a pack of cigarettes still half in the wrapper, and his car keys.

"I've got the flashlight."

He backed out of the cabinet on his hands and knees to accept it. For a moment he fiddled with the flashlight, twisting the front of it to make the scope of the beam widen and narrow. She stood with her arms crossed a few feet from him. When he leaned back into the cupboard she took his wallet from his coat pocket and stuck it in the front pouch of her hoodie. She folded her hands over it, pressing it into her belly.

"Yup, I think I'm seeing the hole. We'll stuff that and see if it solves the problem," he told her.

The landlord emerged from the cabinet.

"Do you have a beer? Just one, I'm driving."

"I don't."

"I haven't gotten rent for March off you yet, do you have that here?" The landlord was pulling out a kitchen chair.

"I don't have it on me right now. I think the steel wool might be under the sink in the bathroom — I'll just check."

She took everything out of the wallet and laid it on the edge of the sink. Seventy bucks in twenties and fives. Some credit cards. Gift cards to Mark's Work Wearhouse and Kent. She put the wallet back together. He would know she took it. Still, she slid the wallet into a folded towel on the shelf behind the door.

"No steel wool in there. We might not have any."

When she came back to the kitchen the landlord was examining the window frame. "Notice any leaking here?" he said.

"I get paid on the fifteenth. I can definitely get you the money then. I can actually give you half of it now, if that's better." She stayed on the other side of the kitchen.

"No, that's fine, I'd rather just collect it all at once. If you don't have the money by the fifteenth we're going to have to have a more serious conversation. Just come look at this window."

She approached the window and he laid a hand on her shoulder and pointed at the frame.

"See the discolouration there? Keep an eye on that for me." He squeezed her shoulder. "If there's any leaking the whole wall could rot out."

"Okay." Mary shifted to get him to take his hand off her and he slid it down her back.

"I've been doing this for a long time. I can tell who might be late once or twice and who is going to fuck off in the middle of the night without paying me. I don't appreciate being left a pile of crap that has to go to the dump—I don't mind calling a lawyer on someone who tries that. I don't think you're the type to fuck someone over but I don't want you to make a habit of lateness." His hand was moving in a slow circle on her lower back.

"I'll definitely have it by the middle of the month."

"You must have got some fright when you saw that rat." He moved his hand down again and cupped her ass. She stepped away.

"Okay, I'm going to run down to the car for that poison. See if you can find the steel wool."

"What if it didn't go back in? It'll get stuck out here when we plug up the hole," she said when he came back.

"I'd say he's back in there. He's probably as scared of you as you are of him." The landlord opened the poison, which came in a small cardboard box. He got on his hands and knees. When he shook the box, dark green pellets tumbled out. Some went into the hole and some landed inside the cupboard.

"You'll need to wear gloves when you clean that up," he said. "Don't touch it with your hands. Get some steel wool and block up the hole, they can't chew through that." Slowly, he got up off the floor. "I'll be back on the fifteenth, probably around suppertime." He lifted his jacket off the back of the chair and left with it under his arm.

When he left she took all the dishtowels out of the drawer with rubber gloves and put them in the washer. Her phone started vibrating on the counter; the words "Greg landlord" lit up the screen again and again. She took the cash out of the long pouch in the back of the wallet. She stuffed the wallet with the cards still in it into the bathroom garbage, down into the used pads and tissues. She put on a hoodie and carried the old garbage that was piled up on the deck down the street and threw it in the alley along with the garbage from the bathroom.

BRITTANY HAD TO be at work in twenty minutes. Thai Express had just opened in the mall and the girls got takeout and ate in the parking lot. Brittany slid a flimsy cup holder out of a slot in the dashboard and fit her drink into it.

"Did the landlord come by for the rent?" Brittany was wearing a black scoop-neck dress with black tights under her winter jacket.

"I talked to him," Mary told her.

"You didn't give him the money?" The tail of Brittany's braid dipped into her takeout container and she flicked it over her shoulder.

"I don't have my half together. But I talked to him about it. He's fine with it."

"I'm going to try and get you a job. One of the servers has an interview at the new place on the waterfront, so there could be an opening for a server. You should apply at that new place too."

"I already applied there. Anyway, don't worry about it. I'll have more shifts at the diner in the summer—tourists love Family Restaurant." Mary was struggling to keep a slippery noodle between the tips of her chopsticks.

"Mary, I don't want to be a dick, but we're going to have to take care of the rent before that. What did you do with my half?"

"It's in the envelope in my room. I wouldn't spend it, God."

Brittany closed the lid of her takeout container and turned the key in the ignition.

WHEN MARY OPENED the door for the landlord she saw that his son was sitting in the passenger seat. He looked about five or six: he had a *Cars* book bag in his lap.

"I left my wallet here when I came about the rat. I called a few times." The landlord was wearing a hat that had earflaps with braided strings hanging from them.

"I haven't seen it." She had been ignoring the landlord's calls for over a week.

"This is the last place I had it."

"I'll call you if I see it." She held out an envelope; she'd made up the last of her half with the cash from his wallet.

"I cancelled all the credit cards, but my licence is in there." He took the envelope from her. "It's all here?" He was looking at her breasts. She caved into herself, drawing her shoulders toward each other in the front.

He put a hand on the doorframe and leaned in. She backed into the dark porch.

"I like you, but I have to draw the line somewhere. I don't want to have to ask you to move out."

"That's all of it," Mary said.

He tore the envelope open. "Any sign of the rat?" he asked, once he'd counted the money.

"I haven't seen it."

"Sounds like we got him. Otherwise he'd be into the food and everything by now. Make sure you put the garbage out on time. Keep the place clean. You don't want him coming back. Okay, I'm gone, I'm taking Evan to a birthday party."

He put the cash back in the envelope, folded it in two, and stuck it in his back pocket.

BRITTANY WANTED TO go to a movie.

"I can't, I'm broke." Mary had spent all the money from Mr. Holloway's daughter on her phone bill.

"Please? I'll pay for it. I made so much in tips last night, it's ridiculous." They were both hungover; there was a bag of chips open on the couch between them. "There was this table of oil executives with company credit cards and they bought six bottles of wine."

"How do you know they were company credit cards?"

"I don't know, business people have company credit cards. Usually, I guess." Brittany turned a bottle of nail polish remover upside down on a wad of toilet paper.

"I could pay you back," Mary said.

She and Brittany were getting fries at Dairy Queen before the movie when she saw the landlord across the food court. His son was walking next to him. The son's cheeks were flushed, his winter coat was open, and he was wearing a hockey jersey. There was a woman with them.

"That's our landlord over there," she told Brittany.

Brittany turned around.

"Don't look at him, I mean don't be obvious, do you think that's his wife?" The woman had on a puffy coat and she had short hair. She was younger than the landlord but older than them.

"I don't care if he sees me," Brittany said. "My half of the rent was ready on time."

Then the girls were at the counter. They ordered the fries and moved to the side to wait for them. The land-lord and his family were lining up at Buck Weavers. He was pointing up at the board. Mary couldn't tell if he was ignoring her or if he hadn't seen her. She saw him take a new wallet out of his back pocket to pay for the sandwiches.

Mary and Brittany sat down at a table and shared the fries from a paper sleeve, dipping them into a paper cup of ketchup. The landlord and his family walked down the wide aisle between the tables.

"Hi there, girls," the landlord said as he passed them.

"Hi," Brittany answered.

He didn't alter his pace. He wasn't embarrassed to see her.

LINDA'S RETURN FLIGHT was delayed and Mary got called in to cover the breakfast/lunch service. She started her shift by collecting all the dirty rags into a milk crate to bring down to the laundry station in the basement.

"Ted wants to see you in the office." The line cook passed with a stack of Costco cheesecake boxes in his arms.

She took the dirty rags with her and left them by the laundry station on her way to the office where her boss tabulated hours and did up the cheques. Ted's chair was against the back wall and his beer gut was pressing up against the edge of the desk. He was wearing a grey polo shirt and had stubble on his face. She stood in the door and he waved her in, motioning her into a chair made of rusty metal tubes and two squares of lacquered plywood.

"I want to show you something." He moved the monitor so she could see it. She leaned forward in the chair and a splinter of plywood dug into her leg.

The screen was divided into four: the porch; the dining room; the area behind the cash, including the register, a bit of the line, and a bit of the dish pit; and the back door, which also showed the laundry station. There was a date at the bottom of the screen, three sets of numbers in bright green divided by slashes. She was too nervous to work out what night they were looking at. She was there in the bottom-right square of the screen, standing behind the cash and tightening her ponytail. She hadn't expected the tapes to be in colour.

"I didn't have a chance to go through this until last night." Her boss pushed a stack of files to the edge of the desk to make sure she could see the screen. "When someone doesn't do the cash that's a red flag for me, I go back and check the tapes. I don't want to assume the worst but I have to look out for myself."

He pressed a button on the screen and fast-forwarded through the night, making Mary speed around the dining room, wiping tables, running food, taking payments. You could see the line cook's hand laying plates at the edge of the line. The dishwasher walked back and forth like Charlie Chaplin with pans of dirty dishes in his arms. In the dining room, customers' arms moved from their plates to their mouths like they were very hungry people in *Looney Tunes*. The top-left square with the back door mostly stayed dark and static.

She was trying to remember the point in the night when she'd started drinking. Ted flew past her stealing the onion ring without comment. He hit the space bar and things slowed to a natural pace. It was the end of her shift. She was filling the mop bucket with the hose from the dish pit. She let the hose flop on its springy coil. Her back was to the camera. Her boss froze the tape.

"What do you have to say about that?" He put his finger on the screen. She was holding a shot glass filled with amber liquid. "People drinking on the job deeply pisses me off. I didn't want to call you in to work today but I had no choice."

If only she hadn't stuck her arm out to the side like that, or she'd moved deeper into the dish pit. She couldn't take her eyes off the floor.

"We're done here. I'll send your cheque and T4s through the mail."

When she got upstairs there were people waiting in the porch to be seated. Her heart was pounding in her chest. She wanted to leave but she needed the sixty bucks she'd make from the shift. The dishwasher made sympathetic eyes at her as he laid a tray of glasses on the counter by the microwave to be shined.

MR. HOLLOWAY SAT in the living room with the TV on while Mary cleaned the bathroom.

"Would you straighten the couch for me?" he asked when he finished his lunch. There were two crocheted blankets on the sofa, mustard and burgundy pucks stitched together at their edges, one draped over the back of the couch and one stretched over the seat. Mr. Holloway hated them to be wrinkled but he didn't have the flexibility to flick the blankets out over the couch and smooth them. While Mary made up the couch, Mr. Holloway got up and left his dishes on the dining room table.

Once he was settled, his tailbone against the back of the couch, his spine curving out past the armrests, he entered some kind of meditative state. She knew he was barely able to hear or see the television, but he liked it being on.

Mary collected the cleaning supplies from under the sink. With the bathroom door open she could see into Mr. Holloway's bedroom. She had looked around in there before; on Fridays she usually washed the bedding. Mrs. Holloway's jewellery box was still on the dresser. Mary lifted the lid and a tiny plastic ballerina on a delicate metal coil sprang up, the first plucks of a melody were churned out before she slammed the lid down. She stripped the bed, heaping the dirty sheets on the floor. There was a small crucifix with a brass Jesus hanging off it above the bed. She pulled open the drawer of the left bedside table. There was a jelly eye-mask, probably belonging to Mrs. Holloway as well, and a Bible. The right bedside table had a chequebook in it. It fit into the deep pocket of her hoodie with just a bit of the cardboard backing sticking out but she put it back in the drawer.

In the bathroom she used cleaning products they didn't keep at her place because of Brittany's allergies and what the chemicals did to the environment. She liked the way the bleach burned her nose. She loved grinding

Comet into the bathtub and then swiping it away to make the bath glare white. You couldn't draw out that blunt, absolute white with the cleaners at her apartment.

Star of the Sea

SINCE THEY'D TORN the hall down, light poured through the back of the house in the morning. Cyril could tell the time of day by where shadows fell on his walls and furniture. Looking out his back windows, he could see right into the lot where the Star of the Sea had been. It was a pit probably twelve feet deep with a chain-link fence around it. There were three bright yellow excavators in the pit.

Those windows had always been filled by the forest green clapboard of the Star of the Sea. All there'd been between it and his house was a narrow strip where a few scrawny trees and a thicket of mile-a-minute grew. During events men had wandered back there to piss. In the afternoon, groups of teenagers had congregated there to smoke in circles with their knapsacks on the ground in front of them. Now he could see across the harbour to the Southside Hills.

Cyril managed a furniture store on Water Street

called Winter's Furniture Emporium. His son Justin worked four days a week; on weekends he worked as a busboy at a club downtown. Mornings when they worked together Cyril would pick Justin up from the apartment where he lived with his girlfriend. A muscular young man named Ron worked full-time. Justin and Ron did all the lifting. Cyril organized the showroom and kept track of inventory; he did all the paperwork and bookkeeping.

He'd been doing it for twenty-six years but it was still hard to predict what would draw people in, what would sell and what wouldn't. He'd found it was worth it to have one outrageous piece in the window, not because someone would buy it but because it would bring in the people who wanted something unique. Unique things were expensive. So he'd usually go with something very distinct and modern, some kind of futuristic recliner and some ol' standbys: a sectional in a stylish, solid colour; a floral couch. There were always people looking for light-coloured floral sofas.

A wrecking ball had taken off the Star of the Sea's roof. He'd watched them unfurling the chain-link fence and affixing the bright plastic signs warning that the hall had become a construction site. They'd hauled out a lot of the inside first and carted it away. The broken ceiling fell down through the floors and took the tops of the walls with it. Cyril hadn't seen the wrecking ball in action; he was at work when they knocked the roof in. He came home and saw through his windows that the walls of the hall were jagged at the top and the roof was gone.

JUSTIN TOLD HIM Brenda was seeing another man. When he heard that, Cyril had to conjure up three lonely Christmases, counting backward on his fingers to figure out how long they'd been separated. It hadn't occurred to him that she might be seeing someone else.

Brenda was a makeup artist. Her friends were movie people and theatre people. They went out for drinks and to events where the men were expected to wear funky, collared shirts under nice sweaters. They loved dinner parties. Cyril hated eating out and he hated hosting.

"Mom's seeing this guy Derek," Justin said. Cyril tried to look unsurprised. Justin had come over for dinner after work. Cyril made them tuna melts and they were eating them with knives and forks on the couch, watching *CSI*. The clock was ticking on the mantel above the couch.

"Me and Meghan might go skiing with him and Mom at White Hills this weekend." Justin pressed on. "And I was wondering if you might be able to take care of Meghan's cat because her roommates are out of town."

"She'll bring over the litter box and everything? I mean, yes, I can do it." Up until this dinner he had believed, without realizing he believed it, that he and Brenda would get back together.

"Great, thanks." Justin cut a square off his soggy tuna melt.

The light shining through the space where the Star of the Sea used to be was bouncing off the white wall behind the television. It made their outlines appear on the screen, on top of a man holding a sealed plastic bag with a shirt in it.

"Should I pull down the blind?" Cyril asked.

"It's not bothering me," Justin said.

Cyril had no idea what was happening in *CSI*. DNA evidence had been found on a plaid shirt but the significance of it was lost on him.

CYRIL WAS STANDING in his living room, looking at the clock his mother had given him and Brenda as a wedding present. It sat under a glass dome and had three gold balls that rotated with the ticking of the seconds.

The clock's glass dome smashed against the floor when he dropped it into the empty garbage bag. Meghan's cat was sleeping in the sun on the windowsill and the sound of the breaking glass startled it awake. Cyril had to go find a box in the basement to put the sharp pieces in so the garbage man wouldn't cut himself.

There were pictures of Justin's ski trip on Facebook. Every member of Cyril's family was tagged in the album, along with Derek Adams. Derek was young—younger than Cyril, anyway. He had all of his hair and it was dark and shiny. He had one of those angular, big-eyed, actor faces. He was wearing some kind of government-issued parka from the seventies in all the outdoor pictures.

There was a photo that Brenda must have taken of Derek and Justin and Meghan drinking hot chocolate in the ski lodge. They all had red cheeks and damp hair. Derek was wearing an eighties sweatshirt with a design of three large pastel triangles on the chest. Meghan was leaning in to hear what Derek was saying. Cyril had lived through the eighties and that kind of sweater had been very unhip.

Cyril thought about the day last summer when he had helped Meghan and Justin move in together. He had driven them back and forth across town, collecting furniture from each of their houses. Cyril only took one day a week off in the summers and it had been a rare hot day in a mostly grey, rainy month.

There'd been a set of crooked stairs leading up to Meghan's old place. Cyril and Justin had to stand the couch up on its arm and flip it completely over three times to get it out the front door. Their T-shirts were wet under the armpits and down the centre of their backs and chests. The couch was covered in matted cat hair, probably five cats' worth. Girls in cutoff jean shorts kept walking by saying, "Don't let the cats out, the cats will try to get out." Nobody had leaned in to hear what Cyril had to say with sweaty-haired exuberance. Apparently he didn't inspire that kind of thing the way Derek did.

FOR A WHOLE weekend after the ceiling had been knocked down, a balcony remained attached to the back wall, reaching out over the sea of rubble. One night some teenagers broke in, crawled through the field of crumbled cement, and set fireworks off on the balcony. The noise woke Cyril up. He went downstairs and saw the Roman candles spitting up over the ragged edges of the hall and

sinking back into the remains. A final celebration. It occurred to him that he should call the fire department or
the police. Instead he put a quilt from the couch around
his shoulders and drank a beer.

There were many fronts he'd failed on. He could have
cleaned the place where the toilet met the floor more
often. He could have made a bigger deal of her birthday;
she loved her own birthday and he found that childish.
He could have gone to more things: the plays she worked
on and the parties for them. He could have responded
more graciously when she sent him the video of a sixty-
year-old porn star explaining the ins and outs of orally
pleasuring a woman.

Brenda had been a friend of Cyril's brother and he'd
seen her around since they were teenagers, though they
didn't get to know each other until they were in their early
thirties. A man had been walking through the fire station
parking lot on Harvey Road with two dogs on leashes.
A car swung into the parking lot and headed straight
toward the dogs. The owner froze and Brenda, who had
been coming from the opposite direction, stepped in front
of the car to save the dogs. The car slowed but not quickly
enough and it rolled over her foot. The tire snapped two
of her bones. Cyril was stopped at the light on Harvey
Road as all of this unfolded. A crowd of pedestrians was
gathering. Even though he hardly knew her, he pulled
out of the traffic to offer her a ride to the Health Sciences.

Brenda had to wear a cast for seven weeks and couldn't
work. Two toes stuck out of the cast and she painted the

nails to match the nails of the healthy foot. They had very careful sex two or three times a day while her foot was healing. He came over on his way to the furniture store and on his way home. She elevated the foot in the cast on the arm of the sofa and rested the other foot on the floor. He kneeled between her open thighs and held her in place by the hips while he went down on her, careful not to knock against her injured foot. After they had sex in the evening he'd make her dinner and wash the dishes. When the cast came off, her foot was small and shrivelled. She climbed on top of him for the first time and they got pregnant.

Justin didn't bring Derek up again until months after the ski trip. It was an unusually slow day at the furniture store; the weather was hot for April and people wanted to be outside. Justin sat in a recliner at the back of the store looking at his phone all afternoon. Cyril had called him in because there was supposed to be a dining room set coming in that needed to be assembled, but it hadn't shown up. At lunchtime he sent Justin down the street to buy them each a sandwich and a drink.

Justin laid his father's sandwich on the counter and walked to the back of the showroom.

"You don't want to eat up here?" Cyril asked.

"I like to be back here where I can't see the sky—it's too depressing seeing how nice it is out when you're stuck in here."

"Well, actually, I'd rather you didn't eat on the furniture."

Justin came up and unwrapped his sandwich on the counter. He laid his phone next to the crumpled Saran Wrap.

"This is Derek's band." Justin pushed the phone toward Cyril. "That's their music video. Mom did all the makeup."

There was a woman on the tiny screen dancing on the hood of a car in an empty parking lot. The cart corral glinted in the moonlight behind her; the camera shook. Cyril picked up the phone and held it close to his face. It looked like the Sobeys on Ropewalk Lane.

"Derek is in this band?"

"Well, it's really Clairissa's band. He just plays bass. Someone else used to play bass, but his girlfriend just had a baby so now Derek's doing it."

"That's Clairissa? You've met her?" Cyril asked. The video cut to a shot of Clairissa lip-synching on a cliff above Middle Cove Beach.

"Yeah, she's really cool, she's from Slovenia," Justin said. The store phone rang and Cyril turned to answer it, gesturing for Justin to mute the video. Justin dropped the Saran Wrap from his sandwich in the garbage and headed to the back of the store.

The dining room set arrived fifteen minutes before they were about to close. Then it turned out the delivery guy had lost an invoice Cyril needed to sign. Justin and Cyril watched through the front window as the delivery guy climbed back into the cab of his truck to talk to his boss privately on the phone. Justin sighed heavily when the delivery guy hung up and dialled a second number.

They ended up getting out a half hour later than usual.

When they got in Cyril's car after finally locking up, it was full of stale, hot air. "Do you want to swing by McDonald's before I drop you home?" Cyril asked.

"Sure." Justin put down his window. "I wanted to talk to you about something."

"Okay." Cyril's first thought was that Justin must need money.

"Derek said he might be able to get me a job doing roadie stuff for his band this summer. They're touring around Atlantic Canada, going to festivals and stuff."

"Well, that sounds exciting." Warm wind rushed through the car.

"I just wanted to let you know because of the store and stuff. It'd be for July and part of August."

Cyril just nodded. He knew it was unfair of him to be hurt that Justin was choosing not to spend the summer with him. He wasn't going to say anything about it to Brenda either. Objecting would only come across as lonely and desperate.

But then he saw her in the section of the supermarket with the home appliances. He was holding a twelve-dollar hand blender; she was a few feet ahead, looking at a box of stemless wineglasses. It was always terrible to see her unexpectedly. She'd had her hair cut since the last time he'd seen her. It was up around her ears with a little tuft of purple in the front. She was wearing the spring jacket she had bought for herself while they were Christmas shopping for Justin a few years ago. She'd almost given the jacket to the Sally Ann when she was cleaning her closet once and he'd begged her not to because he loved what the colour did to her eyes.

"Cyril." She left her cart and walked toward him.

"Derek asked Justin to go on tour," he said, surprising himself.

"I know," Brenda said. "It's a job, Cyril. It can get him other jobs, and it's a chance to travel." The jacket was light purple, faded almost to grey. He knew she was keeping it because of what he'd said.

"He told me he'd be helping out at the store this summer. He made a commitment." These were also things he had decided not to say.

"Cyril, please don't take this personally. It's a chance for Justin to see the country and to be involved in the music scene. That's exciting for him."

"I can't hold the job is all. I'll have to hire someone else. The job won't be there when he gets back."

"I'm sure he'll understand." Brenda put the glasses in her cart. Cyril realized she was ending the conversation.

"I don't think I'm going to get this." He put the blender back on the shelf.

"Have a good day, Cyril." She stepped behind her cart and pushed it around him, continuing down the aisle.

Cyril needed olive oil, but he went straight to the checkout to avoid running into her again.

THE STAR OF the Sea had been rented out for weddings almost every weekend in the summer. The music from the receptions would flood the house whenever someone pushed their way out of the heavy double doors on the side of the hall. People were always pouring out of the emergency exits to smoke.

When Brenda was still there they had the dining room table in the back room. Brenda liked sitting with the windows open, listening to the bits of drunken conversation that sailed into the house.

She would angle her chair so she could see the girls' outfits in the sliver of the street that was visible from the back of the house. She'd put her feet up on the table and lean back so the chair stood on its hind legs.

The receptions went late into the night. Each gush of music was bookended by the bang of the steel doors meeting in their frame. He remembered being woken up by bursts of "Girls Just Want to Have Fun" and lying awake with Brenda's cheek resting on his bare chest. They'd kicked the blankets to the end of the bed; her bare ass on the flowery sheets, a hoarse chorus of wedding guests wailing *"They just wanna."* After she left, he had that memory every time he was woken up by a wedding reception.

Now there was never music in the night on his street. In the morning there was construction-site noise. The shrill beeping of large vehicles reversing, rubble raining into the back of a dump truck.

"Do you still have that backpack we took camping in

Gros Morne when I was a kid?" Justin asked him one afternoon at the store. They were on their hands and knees screwing the legs into a mahogany table that could seat twelve.

"What backpack?" Cyril stood up for a moment to try to stretch stiffness out of his lower back.

"It was light blue with an aluminum frame. I was wondering if I could take it on tour."

"I think it's in the basement. You can take it if you can find it," Cyril said. Things had been decided; he would have to look for a new guy to help Ron with deliveries.

Meghan came for the drive to the airport and Cyril was dreading having to make conversation with her on the way back. It was so bright outside that when he first went through the doors of the terminal it took his eyes a moment to adjust to the dimness.

Brenda was there. Because of the light, he was only two feet away when he finally recognized her. She'd dropped Derek off and was waiting to give Justin a hug goodbye. Derek and the rest of the band were already halfway through the check-in line. The woman from the video was wearing sunglasses and leather boots that came up over her knees. Cyril thought of a shot from the video where she was squirming on white sheets. He wondered how Brenda felt about Derek going off with the woman. But then, Justin would be there.

Cyril and Brenda went to get coffees to give Meghan and Justin privacy while they hugged goodbye.

"I heard they're tearing down the Star of the Sea," Brenda said in the coffee line.

"It's gone, it's been gone for months," Cyril told her.

"It's torn down?"

"Haven't you driven past?"

"I guess I haven't. What are they putting there?"

"Something hideous. A parking garage. But right now the house is full of light. I can see the Southside Hills."

Brenda and Cyril and Meghan walked out of the terminal together. When they got to the curb, Brenda headed off toward her own car. Cyril thought about how, before Justin got his own place, Brenda would sometimes stop in when she was picking him up or dropping him off. Cyril wished there was a reason for her to stop in now, so he could show her how the absence of the hall changed the house.

He missed her things. Her makeup cases, from the outside, looked like toolboxes. They were designed the same way on the inside too: a shallow top shelf divided into small compartments that reached halfway out over the deeper, undivided bottom compartment. The wide bottom held fat tubs of concealer, brushes tucked into protective sleeves and lipsticks in metal tubes. The smaller compartments held the delicate, glittery things: the false eyelashes and adhesive gems. She made old people young for interviews and young people old for movies and plays. When Justin was in junior high she'd helped do him up as Ace Frehley from KISS for Halloween. When he wiped the makeup off his face that night, Cyril noticed for the first time that Justin was beginning to look like a teenager.

Before Cyril left for work the next morning he watched them pour the foundation of the parking garage. The wet concrete had the thick, gluey consistency of oatmeal.

Lucky Ones

SHERRY WAS TAKING care of her boyfriend Mike's baby so he could pick up an extra shift. Mike worked at the Weston bread factory. He liked it there. He said there were tea and cookies in the break room. They got dental. His sweat smelled of warm dough, it was like he was always sweating off a hangover.

Beth's mother dropped her off around suppertime. Sherry recognized the ancient alchemy at work in Beth's face. The way the baby was both of them, this woman and Mike, and neither of them.

The mother laid the diaper bag and car seat on the sidewalk. She carried her daughter into Sherry's house and Sherry followed with the seat in her arms and the bag on her shoulder. They passed the wall of empties in the front porch. Sherry could smell the cat's litter and also the yeast smell Mike brought home with him.

In the kitchen Beth took slow steps toward the cat,

who was asleep in a square of sun on the linoleum floor.

"How about we take a little walk over to the store?" Sherry asked as soon as she was alone with the little girl. She lifted Beth up by the armpits. The baby's eyes weren't dark like Mike's at all; they were her mother's dull blue.

Beth had the same wide nostrils as her dad but on her face they looked fragile. She had his see-through eyelashes. She had his fine red hair too, but on her it was a mess of tangled curls. The way she was and wasn't him reminded Sherry of a party trick. Like wiggling your body through a metal hanger or flipping your eyelids inside out.

Sherry put on a pair of flip-flops by the front door and headed over to the store. Beth's baby pot-belly was pressed against her side. Cars stopped in both directions to let them cross Queen's Road. It was evening. People were turning on their headlights. Sherry felt the cold on her ankles.

She tapped the top shelf of the Nevada case with her knuckle.

"Five of those." The baby's pale eyelashes dipped down and slowly rose up again. Beth was holding the neck of Sherry's shirt in both hands. She was getting sleepy.

"Five of those." Sherry tapped the second shelf. "And ten of the bottom."

"Five, five, ten?"

"See if you can pick me out some lucky ones," Sherry said.

The cashier tossed one on top of the other until they were a little cardboard heap on the counter.

Beth was sitting on the counter. Sherry would be able to see Mike pull up in front of their house through the front door of the store. She handed the cashier a twenty. She lifted up one of her wads of tickets. She bent the first ticket until its back buckled and the little tabs sprang open. Nothing. She bent the second one. Nothing. Beth was holding a bag of candy in each hand. The baby brought her hands together and made the bags smash against each other.

"She's the spit of Mike, she's got his face," the cashier said.

The twelfth ticket. Fifty dollars. Three gold bells tilted on their sides, singing out.

"Got it."

The cashier turned the key and the cash slid open. Ten, twenty, twenty.

"You're a lucky charm," Sherry said, rubbing Beth's belly. She picked up the next ticket. Nothing. Nothing. Nothing. Sherry leaned back to see if Mike's car had pulled up.

"Five more of the bottom." She handed the cashier one of her new twenties. It was soft like it'd been through the wash. Nothing. Nothing. Nothing.

Sherry's jeans were tight and she could feel the new twenty and ten scrunched in her front pocket along with some change. She took the baby back across the road to her little apartment.

Sherry made macaroni and cheese for Beth. She melted a hunk of butter and sprinkled grated cheese into it and whipped it with a fork. She sat Beth in her booster seat and snapped the tray into place.

Beth dug her hands into the bowl and mashed warm macaroni into her scalp. She ground the white noodles and the sauce into her red curls. She looked Sherry right in the eyes while she did it.

The baby fell asleep on the couch. There was still some crusty macaroni close to her scalp. She had fallen asleep with her head in Sherry's lap and her knees drawn up to her belly. Sherry picked the little scabs of melted cheese out of the baby's hair. The light of the store's sign made the living room curtains glow yellow. She eased Beth's head onto the sofa and went to the window and parted the curtain. She could see the cashier hunched over a paper he'd spread out on the ice cream cooler.

Sherry dragged two chairs in from the kitchen and set them up with their backs to the edge of the couch. There was no way the baby could roll off.

The street was empty. Sherry got in line behind some girls whose taxi was idling outside the store. They were bleached and tanned and made-up. They wanted this type of cigarettes and then that type and the key to the beer cooler. The cashier was asking did they have ID. The girls opened their suitcase-sized purses and started taking things out and laying them on the counter. Sherry could see the light on in her living room from where she stood in line.

She spent the last of her new money. She got a big stack of tickets.

"See if you can pick me out some lucky ones," she told the cashier.

They were so light in her hands. She gave half the pile to the cashier to open. A line of cherries. Sherry ripped the tabs off the last one and laid the ticket on the counter.

"Five bucks."

Mike's car pulled in where the taxi had just pulled out. She saw him see her through the glass in the door. There was no way the baby could roll off that couch. She still had the bottom half of her stack to get through.

Dead Skin

AFTER THE FIRST FROST, me and Rick Fowler walked up to the barrens. It was late afternoon, we'd just tried out for the Junior Boys' basketball team. The grass on the hill had turned yellow and the wind was brushing it flat against the damp mud. From there you could see the whole community. The familiar swish of Kent's Road sliding down the hill. The wide stretch of fissured pavement where Kent's Road met up with Trestle Road. Both ends of Beach Road, cut off with sawhorses that had been spray-painted a watery neon orange by the town council. The choppy sea belted by a grey horizon.

Rick Fowler was wearing a windbreaker with a pocket in the front of it. I could smell the syrupy, medicinal smell of a cough drop on his breath.

"Just 'cause I'm short doesn't mean I can't jump high though," I was telling Rick.

"Look at Brad, he's second-tallest in the class but he

can't get an inch off the ground," Rick said.

My sneaker slid out from underneath me and my knee went into the grass and sank into the damp mud beneath it. When I stood up my jeans clung to that part of my knee. The fabric was soaked and gritty.

Rick wanted to show me something. He pointed to a stand of pitcher plants bowing toward the ground.

"That's where we're going, over there."

"What? Over by the stream?"

"Over by the flowers."

The ground was spongy by the stream. Rick Fowler was wearing rubber boots but I had my sneakers on from tryouts still.

Rick took out his knife and sliced the head of a pitcher plant off its leathery stalk. His cheeks were red from the cold and there was a glimmer of clear mucus sliding out of one of his nostrils. He passed me the knife and held the flower between his thumb and forefinger. Each petal was a neat triangle and they all folded in on themselves, an envelope. Rick picked them apart. Inside the flower was a pockmarked, frozen globe. Three mosquitoes were suspended in the ice. Their gangly legs frozen mid-gallop.

"I dare you to eat this," he said.

"Okay. I don't care."

"Open your mouth."

Rick Fowler put the ball of ice on my tongue. I felt the cold lump slide down the back of my throat.

"Did you swallow it? Open your mouth."

I opened my mouth and stuck my tongue out. We

could hear the growl of quads tearing around the woods but they were far off. When I put my tongue back in my head he put his lips on my lips. And then he put his hands on my hips. He got on his knees and lifted up the bottom of my padded vest and put his lips there. We kept going like that. Lips and hands and the little ball melting in my stomach. He took me apart, lifted my skin off.

I could feel the wind coming in from the choppy sea and stroking my muscles. My body was an elastic-band ball of muscles pulled taut. Some places in my face there was just bone with nothing on it. Not smooth or shiny or polished. It didn't gleam when the sun hit it. Just dried out, almost soft, grey-white bone. I could touch my brain. It was dark and damp and wrinkled like a fingerprint.

Then we walked home. My pants were soaked from being on the ground. I held my skin up to keep it from dragging in the mud on the way down the hill.

I called Rick Fowler once. From a pay phone in Toronto.

"How's everything back home? What's all the news?" I asked him.

"They've got President's Choice chicken wings in garlic and honey sauce at the store now. Just got wireless Internet here. We were the last place to get cell-phone reception on the shore. I got a new dog, a little puppy."

Hearing his voice made me remember things about home I hadn't realized I'd forgotten.

"I'm thinking about coming home," I said.

"You don't want to do that. You're settled up there.

There's nothing here worth coming back for."

I picked my skin off the floor of the phone booth, climbed back into it, and walked to my narrow apartment. I lived above a takeout place with my boyfriend. It was a damp night and my skin started losing the flaky, dried-out feel, suctioning into all the crevices, tightening around the backs of my knees and ears. I wasn't really thinking about moving home. My boyfriend was at the library writing a paper due the next morning. He'd left with a travel mug of coffee and a handful of granola bars.

At home I got in bed and listened to the takeout place downstairs closing up. I knew the sounds of the end of their night by heart, from the mop bucket being filled to the door rocking in its frame when they rattled it to make sure it was locked. The familiar song of the takeout place locking up for the night put me to sleep.

Barrelling Forward

"YOU OKAY?" Kyle asked his sister. They were at the ferry terminal, in a line of idling cars.

"I'm okay."

"Maybe you're hungry."

"Maybe we shouldn't use the money, Kyle," Shawna said.

"We're only using a small amount of the money."

"I'm just saying maybe we should put it away. I want to use mine to go to university. That's what Mom would have wanted me to do with it."

"I'm going to get a job. You can get a job too, if you want. We're only using a little bit. Why don't you have a sandwich?"

Kyle twisted around and lifted a sandwich out of a tray in the back seat, trying not to wake the dog. Their mother's sister had insisted they take the sandwiches from the wake. The triangles of sandwich had been squeezed into a tight ring along the perimeter of the tray, but at some point the dog had stepped on the clear plastic lid and mashed half of them into a gooey mess. Kyle took a stack of curried chicken salad out of the intact side. He tilted the tray toward his sister.

"There's going to be nothing to eat on the boat."

"Yes there will."

"These will go bad if we don't eat them."

There was greenish chicken salad all over his hand. Kyle let the dog lick the seasoned mayonnaise off his fingers.

THE FERRY LURCHED in the windstorm.

Shawna and Kyle were sleeping on a bench below a sign saying to please not sleep on the benches. There was a safety video on a loop on the TV bolted to the wall of the lounge and it crackled in and out of her dreams. *In the event of, arms folded over your chest, equipped with a whistle, inflatable slide.* Dishes crashed in the kitchen.

A man in a chef's coat walked carefully through the lounge holding a stainless-steel restaurant tub. She smelled boiled hot dogs. The boat nosed its way over the peak of a wave and yellow water sloshed out of the hot dog tub. It darkened the front of his uniform and splattered on the floor.

The chef saw her open her eyes and said, "That's it for the dogs, too messy out there, we're shutting down the kitchen."

She and Kyle took turns with the sleeping bag. She

unzipped it and held the corners against her chest. Rolled over and pulled it over her face. No matter how she lay, the blanket kept flopping off her.

"When we wake up you'll be able to see North Sydney," Kyle told her.

Her friends back in St. John's were studying for their final exams. They were eating popcorn and scrolling through Facebook and making up mnemonics for the parts of the somatic nervous system.

"Poor Nanaimo," Shawna said. A woman who worked on the boat had made them lock the dog in a metal kennel on the deck because they didn't have a muzzle for him.

"He'll be all right, go to sleep." Kyle sat up and drew his knees into his chest.

But the storm was keeping her awake. People lined up at the bathroom door and the crew handed out white paper bags lined with shiny foil. A woman stepped away from the bathroom line, vomited into her bag then straightened up. The bottom of the bag sagged and she held it away from herself. Then she pulled it open and bent over again.

"I wish she would go away," Shawna said. The retching noise was making her sick. Kyle scratched her scalp, something they'd done for each other since they were small.

"She can hear you," he said quietly to her.

When the boat arrived in Nova Scotia they had to wait in the belly of the ferry for the drawbridge to come down. There were transport trucks on either side of their tiny car. Shawna turned around in her seat and fed the dog

Goldfish crackers from the glovebox. He licked the little salt crystals off her fingers, his big thick tongue the same pink as a pencil eraser.

"You know what else is great about Montreal? You'll probably pick up some French. If we're there for a while you could become bilingual, that's great for when you're looking for jobs." Kyle watched the cars in front of them, his hands at ten and two on the steering wheel, ready to tap the gas when they started moving.

"I don't want to be there for 'a while.' I need to finish school." Shawna whipped back around and settled into her seat.

"You're *going* to finish school, and you'll go to university. This is a little break," Kyle said. A slice of blue sky appeared and widened as the drawbridge on the back of the boat lowered. The line of cars juddered along the long metal grate that stretched between the edge of the boat and solid land.

Kyle had gone to her school and talked to them. He'd met with her principal and a grief counsellor while she sat out in the hall. They'd postponed her exams until the fall. When Kyle told her the tests were moved, she felt everything she knew begin to seep out of her. Stuff about math formulas, the names of parts of the nervous system, facts about leaders of different countries — all of it started slipping away like a nosebleed. She left her schoolbooks in Newfoundland.

THEIR MOTHER HAD driven into a low cement wall that surrounded someone's property. She'd come around a turn and plowed into it on the way home from a party.

She was in the hospital unconscious with a head injury for three long days. The dress she'd worn to the party was draped over the back of the visitor's chair. It smelled smoky and Shawna realized her mother must have been standing next to a barbecue at the party.

The doctors said there was a chance she would die but Shawna hadn't believed it. The whole time her mother was in the hospital Shawna fantasized about saying, "The doctors said you might not wake up, do you know how that made me feel?"

Their mother drove like that all the time and usually it was fine. She'd grown up in a community where there were no buses or taxis and if you had to get home after having a few drinks, she'd told them, no one batted an eye about you taking the car.

Once when it was hot and they had the windows in the front of the house open, Shawna and Kyle heard the screeching grind of metal on metal and ran out to the front step. Their mother had run the side of the car along a signpost just outside their house. She was sitting with the car door flung open, untangling herself from the seatbelt. When the seatbelt recoiled into the car, she reached for her purse on the passenger seat and held it against her breasts.

"I'm shook up, Kyle. You're going to have to park for me," she called into the road.

She twisted the keys out of the ignition and held them out to him, but stayed in the driver's seat with her legs in the street until Shawna came around to help her. When they brought her inside the smell of beer on her was like the stink of a wet dog.

WHEN THEY ARRIVED in Montreal, Shawna's butt ached from sitting in the car and her clothes were sweaty and stale. Kyle's friend Lonnie led them behind his house into a little garden. There was a mirror with a curved slice missing from the top corner leaning against the back fence. There were white plastic deck chairs with empty beer cans gathered around their legs. Shawna's duffle bag was chafing her shoulder.

Lonnie opened a door at the back of the house to a set of fire-escape stairs going up to his second-floor balcony. The stairs were enclosed to keep snow and ice off them in the winter.

"The last guy who lived in my apartment built this weird little nook in here," Lonnie said as they trooped up behind him.

A doorway at the top of the stairs opened onto Lonnie's balcony. Shawna saw a platform had been built between the roof of the fire-escape enclosure and the top of the doorframe.

"You just move this over here," Lonnie said. He leaned a homemade ladder against the edge of the platform. "It's like an indoor treehouse-slash-loft kind of thing."

The platform was a few sheets of plywood supported by two-by-fours. Lonnie and Shawna stepped onto the balcony to give Kyle some room to climb the ladder.

Kyle paused at the top of the ladder and turned to look down at Shawna and Lonnie. The base of the ladder was not far from the edge of the stairs.

"You think this place can handle both of us?" Kyle asked, heaving his upper body into the loft.

Shawna noticed that the plywood bowed under his weight when he climbed in. She was leaning a hip against the doorframe looking up at Kyle but she was aware of Lonnie's eyes skimming up the length of her body.

"Oh, totally. Me and Patty used to sleep up there all the time," Lonnie said.

"We're going to get our own place soon," Kyle said.

"Stay as long as you want, man."

Shawna climbed up the ladder to the platform. There was a mattress made up with sheets and a sleeping bag. There was a little shelf built into the wall with candles melted onto it and a flashlight with a rubber loop for your wrist.

In places she could see streaks of sky between the boards. Drips of tar had slid through the ceiling and stiffened before they could drop onto the platform. They were frozen mid-drip, covered in grey dust.

"One of you could sleep on my couch too," Lonnie said.

"I think this is good. Nanaimo can sleep down there, at the top of the stairs—that way we'll hear him whining if he needs to pee in the night," Kyle said. "We'll look for our own place as soon as I find a job."

"I'm really sorry about your mom," Lonnie said.

"Thanks, man," Kyle answered.

Shawna glanced over the edge of the platform and down the fire escape. She got a rush of vertigo, she thought of the ferry crashing down from the peak of a wave. She'd seen a woman on the boat hurrying her daughter to the washroom. The floor had come up and she'd had to drop the girl's hand to brace herself against a carpeted wall. Her knee had jutted forward and Shawna saw the outline of her kneecap through her polyester skirt.

Lonnie left them alone to try to organize their things in the narrow bunk.

"We can't keep our bags in here, there's not enough room," Shawna said.

"They're going to have to stay in the house," Kyle agreed.

"We're going to be back for September, right?" Shawna was kneeling on her sleeping bag. Her face was close to her brother's.

"If you still want to at the end of the summer we'll definitely go back."

The dog was whimpering at the bottom of the ladder.

THE FIRST DAYS in Montreal, Shawna spent a lot of time walking around with the dog. She walked from St-Henri to Parc Ex and back. She got sunburnt and didn't eat. She ached with an anxiety that felt like a wet gym sock full of tennis balls twirling in her chest.

One afternoon she was walking downtown and there were students protesting tuition hikes and a new unconstitutional law. She'd heard they were students but there were also grey-haired women in MEC hiking gear and yoga pants, young fathers with little boys on their shoulders. The boys beat their fathers' chests with their sandals.

The wave of people blocked traffic. Drivers smoked cigarettes through cracked windows and sent text messages as they waited for the protest to move on. Some honked and made a show of smiling, or held felt squares that seemed to be a symbol of the protest out the windows. Other drivers tried not to make eye contact, looking neutrally into their laps as people trailed their fingers and banners over their windshields.

Their mother had looked bloated in the coffin. Her cheeks were puffed like she'd just had dental work done. Someone had straightened her hair and sprayed it into stiff wisps. Kyle put an arm around Shawna's shoulders and steered her away. It was only after he'd led her away from the coffin that Shawna realized there was a moan coming out of her. She felt stranded somewhere between being awake and asleep; two worlds were rubbing together and the noise coming from her was a kind of static electricity. She couldn't keep the moan from coming out and it turned into a high coyote whine.

She walked along with the crowd because it felt good for her feet to be in tandem with its rhythm, even though the lonely feeling pulsed in her forehead like a headache, a separate, private beat.

Riot police stood elbow to elbow in every alley. They had straight faces and shields made of scratched Plexiglas. People turned and smiled we're-all-in-this-together smiles at each other and raised their eyebrows and she did the same. There was a whisper about tear gas lapping through the crowd. People started tying bandanas and T-shirts over their mouths and noses. Shawna felt her eyeballs sting, then there were tears in her ears and on her neck; they were making the collar of her T-shirt damp. People around her started running, people were tripping and knocking into each other. She tightened her grip on Nanaimo's leash and shouldered her way out of the crowd.

Back in the loft her calves ached and her stomach felt like it had a high vaulted ceiling.

LONNIE GOT KYLE a job with him at Compost Montréal. The nights were hot and Kyle borrowed one of Lonnie's sweatshirts with the sleeves cut off to wear to work. Sometimes the shirt would shift so far to one side that you could see one of his nipples.

They got home at six each morning with the stink of compost on them. They were full of rambunctious energy from the exertion of lifting the compost bins over their heads again and again, riding through the city all night on the back of a dump truck. Shawna was always woken up by the sound of Lonnie's door slamming when they came in. Next she'd hear knapsacks full of tall cans hitting the kitchen counter, followed by the snap of beers opening on the balcony below the loft. Shawna fantasized about yelling at them to shut up but she couldn't because it was Lonnie's place and they were staying there for free. Instead she would bend her knees and shift her hips until she could close the lip of her sleeping bag over her head. She would stay cocooned until she ran out of air in the suffocating, pitch-black heat and had to stick her head back out into the noise.

KYLE HAD HIS twenty-fourth birthday a couple of weeks before their mother's accident. He'd come over for dinner with Shawna and their mother before going downtown with his co-workers.

Shawna had made macaroni and cheese with bread-crumbs on top, pouring cheese sauce she'd made from scratch over the noodles. Her mother was running out to pick up a cake at Sobeys. Shawna tried to convince her to get something funny written in icing on top.

"Like what?" Their mother spoke in a hushed voice because Kyle was asleep on the couch in the living room. He had lain down on the couch as soon as he got in the door and seemed to fall asleep instantly. He worked over-night as a security guard at a twenty-four-hour pharmacy. He had moved in with one of his co-workers, into a gross little second-floor apartment downtown. Shawna had only been there once, on the day she and their mother helped move his stuff in.

"I don't know, something like 'Happy Birthday, Loser'?" Shawna whispered back, stirring the noodles with a spoon to evenly distribute the cheese sauce.

"Jesus, Shawna, we can't all be honour students. Don't be so hard on your brother." Their mother picked her keys up off the counter.

She had meant it as a silly joke.

Their mother was still at the store when Kyle woke up. Shawna was folding a load of laundry on the kitchen table. Kyle's face was puffy and there was a line on his cheek because he'd been lying on a place where two couch cushions met. Seeing his face swollen with sleep made her miss the three of them living together.

"Smells good." Kyle pulled out a chair.

Shawna opened the oven door a crack to look at the macaroni; she was afraid of the breadcrumbs burning.

"How's Mom?" Kyle asked.

"Not good. When she's not at work she sits on the couch all day in that grubby fleece she used to wear to rake the yard."

"Carol hasn't been around?" Carol was their aunt.

"Carol comes over but they just get drunk together. It's so annoying." Shawna balled up a pair of socks and tossed them onto the pile.

"One more year of school and you'll be able to get your own place," Kyle said.

Her mother came back holding the cake tray with both hands. There was a liquor-store bag digging into her forearm. Shawna was surprised by how angry she felt. No occasion was sacred: every celebration was an excuse to get openly shit-faced.

Shawna had already set three plates out on the table.

"Happy birthday," Shawna said, ladling a splash of macaroni onto her brother's plate.

"Who's going to help me celebrate?" Her mother was taking wine glasses down from the top shelf of the cupboard.

"I will," Kyle said, lifting a forkful of macaroni.

A SINKHOLE HAD opened in the middle of Ste-Catherine after a demo passed. Shawna saw footage of it on a plasma screen in the convenience store.

She had an empty margarine container in her knapsack that she'd found under Lonnie's sink. She filled it with water from the store bathroom, but it couldn't hold its shape with the water in it. She had to set it on the palm of one hand and pinch the rim. Even then, water slopped over the side. She concentrated on the glass doors where the dog was sitting and waiting for her as she tiptoed across the store with the dripping container.

The guy behind the counter ran around and held the door open for her with an outstretched arm. He had slicked black hair and a little spray of freckles near the corner of his left eye. She had to pass close to his chest to get through the door and she breathed in the smell of his cologne and his sweat.

He smelled the way her uncles, her mother's brothers, smelled. At the funeral they had each hugged her in front of the corkboard of photographs of her mother. Someone had tied a purple bow around the corner of the corkboard and propped it on an easel: her mother's graduation photo, her mother and brother in the hospital just after Shawna was born, the three of them in the backyard the day they got Nanaimo.

She sat on the step of the convenience store and watched the dog lap up the water. If she were in Newfoundland she would be writing a biology quiz. She tried to summon the components of the somatic nervous system. Spinal Nerves, Cranial Nerves, Association Nerves. Sometimes Cold & Alone, Sloppy Coors Light Again, Spattered Car Autopsy, Selfish Cunt Suicide.

She walked to the sinkhole. She and Nanaimo stood at the edge of the chain-link fence. The road had crumbled into itself and left a muddy mouth in the middle of a main thoroughfare.

SHAWNA WOKE UP in the night, thirsty and needing to pee. She and Kyle slept side by side with their clothes on in the loft. She had to crawl, feeling for the edge of the platform and then the top of the ladder. Without daylight coming in between the boards of the walls it was completely black in the tight space. A dense, still heat was trapped between the mattress and ceiling.

Making her way down the ladder, she thought of Jim Kennedy, a little kid she had been tutoring in math before they left Newfoundland. Jim Kennedy had dark hair and big blue eyes. Sometimes he would grind his teeth and threaten to crack his pencil in two when he was frustrated. He would put his thumbs together on the centre of the pencil and push upward until she said his name sharply and then he would lay the pencil down. He had short pudgy limbs and sometimes Shawna wanted to hug him to her chest and put her cheek on his head but he was a tiny bit too grown-up for that. Shawna couldn't remember what day of the month it was but he was probably done with the math unit they'd been working on.

One warm evening she found Kyle and Lonnie drinking in the backyard.

"Take the dog out with me," Shawna said to Kyle.

"Just let me finish this beer."

"I'm leaving now."

Her brother put the can down. Lonnie shrugged at him.

They walked to the Plateau, where people were coming out onto their balconies and beating pots with wooden spoons. It made a tinkling noise somewhere between wind chimes and the sound of a waitress dropping a dishpan. There was a girl with a thick blond braid and a set of crutches leaning in a doorframe. She was wearing sweatpants with the band rolled down so you could see the elastic of her underwear against her tanned pelvic bones. She tapped a pot lid against a wooden crutch.

They came across some people singing from sheet music in front of a café. The song was in French but it sounded like an Irish hymn Shawna had learned in school. The wind made the sheets shiver. Shawna and Kyle stood at the edge of the group and Shawna leaned against her brother. He put an arm around her and rubbed her back. A gust of wind hit the photocopied music and the sheets billowed in people's hands, threatening to rip down the centre. Kyle's hand on her back in this little cluster of people reminded her of the funeral.

"I can't get warm," she told him.

"It was so hot today; maybe you have sunstroke."

"I don't have sunstroke. Kyle, I'm afraid we could inherit what Mom had."

"It's not like that. It's a combination of things. A shitty life wears you down. That's why we're here. In a city where there's stuff going on."

"Maybe we're more susceptible."

"Let's not get bogged down in that."

There were about twenty people walking in twos down the road, slamming kitchenware together over their heads. A young man was in front, marching backward so he faced the parade and chanting through a megaphone at the small crowd. He had dreads in a ponytail tied with a red rag; he waved at Shawna and Kyle as he passed them and they each lifted a hand in a show of support. The crowd whooped and banged their pots in response.

WHEN THEY GOT back from the Plateau, Lonnie was in front of the house with a bunch of camping stuff he'd found propped against a Salvation Army donation bin. Everything was wrapped in layers of gummy duct tape.

He said he wanted to go camping in New Hampshire.

"That tent is probably mouldy," Shawna said.

She picked up a small camping lamp that was attached to a set of tent poles by a snarl of tape. The sun was starting to set earlier; their shadows were creeping up the side of the house.

"Don't be so bougie," Lonnie said to her. "My friend just got back from this place called Franconia Notch. They got there after the park closed and they didn't have to pay the campsite fee. They said it was beautiful."

"Parts of that tent are probably missing—are there pegs anywhere?" Shawna said.

"You don't need pegs, you can use sticks." Kyle started picking up the gear to carry into the house.

That night after Lonnie left for work, Shawna and Kyle got out their duffle bags and shoved their dirty laundry into a garbage bag to take to the Laundromat.

"I don't think we should go to New Hampshire—we should be getting ready to go home." Shawna was holding the mouth of the garbage bag open so her brother could shake underwear and socks out of the bottom of his bag into it. "And what would we do with Nanaimo?"

"We'll take Nanaimo with us. There's nothing to get ready, Shawna. The day we decide to go we just have to throw our stuff in the car," Kyle said.

"I need to go back to school in the fall. And we should check on the house." She knotted the top of the garbage bag.

"There's another month until school starts. You should try to meet people, make some friends."

THEY LEFT LONNIE'S at six in the morning to pick up Adalene, a girl who also worked at the compost place. She was standing in front of her apartment with a shopping bag of food and a sleeping bag at her ankles.

Adalene got in the back seat and opened a bag of chips even though it wasn't even eight in the morning yet. The sky still had a hint of pink. They were All Dressed ripple chips and everyone's fingers got covered in rust-coloured dust. The dog slept with his head in Shawna's lap, drooling on her cutoffs.

They spent the day on small highways, driving through little towns and stretches of farmland. They stopped at gas stations that sold fully automatic rifles and had taxidermied animals mounted on the walls.

Lonnie brought up the protests.

"They corral people like cattle. They close in on a chunk of the crowd with their shields and just arrest them all. You know Timmy? Who was over the other night? He got knocked out with a billy club. He was completely unconscious in the road."

Kyle was nodding.

"Have you seen that video of the cops tipping over all the tables on a bar patio? Just going nuts with pepper spray on people, who are like just sitting down drinking beer?"

"Oh yeah, that was fucked," Lonnie said. "My friend Steph saw that happen. She said it was fucked."

"Do they sell beer in convenience stores here?" Kyle asked.

The campsite was in a valley between two mountains.

The seasons rolled back on themselves as they drove down into the valley. The air cooled and there were fewer and fewer leaves on the trees. Kyle put the windows up. A navy blue shadow slipped down the snow-capped mountains as the sun set.

It was dark when they got the tent unravelled. They'd spent too long in the supermarket, where you could get thirty beers for sixteen bucks, Jell-O trays in the shape of the American flag, and marshmallows as big as your fist. As they'd stood in the chill of the beer cooler Lonnie said, "Live free or die, baby."

On the highway they'd seen apple trees in blossom but here, in the valley, the ground was covered in crunchy leaves. She and Adalene set up the tent while Lonnie made a fire. Her brother looped Nanaimo's leash around the leg of the picnic table. After clipping the dog on, Kyle sat down and opened a beer.

"Getting started are ya, Kyle?" Adalene called out. She turned toward Shawna but her headlamp shone right into Shawna's eyes and she had to look away.

"This beer is like water," Kyle answered from the dark.

"That's why it's so cheap, it's like two percent, I bet," Lonnie said, tucking a twisted knot of newspaper in under a pile of sticks.

Shawna finished feeding the first pole through the fabric and the curved backbone of the tent rose up, giving them a sense of the circumference of their shelter. "Are we all going to fit in here?" Adalene asked.

THE GROUND AROUND the fire glittered with crunched beer cans. Adalene and Kyle had been inching toward each other and now their shoulders were touching. There was no wind in Franconia Notch. Lonnie was rolling a joint in his lap. He shredded the weed on a piece of cardboard from the wiener package. Even in the dark the mountains were blue. Shawna could feel the heat of the fire through the rubber soles of her sneakers.

"You're going to burn your shoes, Shawna," her brother said. Adalene had her hand on her brother's thigh and his hand was covering hers.

"I'm going to pee." Shawna got up. The woods were sparse. She had to walk a ways to find a tree big enough to hide her. She squatted, took her shorts down, and swivelled them around an ankle. She had to put a palm against the ground to steady herself. The dirt was cold. She had looked away when they lowered the coffin into the ground. When she was done she leapt up and pee trickled down her leg and onto her sock. She tried to pull her shorts up but her hands were shaking. Her sock was warm and wet.

She rushed back to the campsite and saw Lonnie by himself at the edge of the fire. He was gently poking a stick up through a piece of white bread, holding the bag with the rest of the loaf between his skinny knees. He paused with the slice halfway impaled to take a sip of beer.

"They went for a walk. I'm making toast."

She sat down next to him and Lonnie slapped a hand on her knee.

"Should I roll another joint?"

"I'm going to sleep," Shawna said, as she jerked her leg out from under his heavy fingers. She felt completely sober.

She crossed the campsite and crawled into the mouth of the tent. Nanaimo was curled up on her brother's sleeping bag; his ears perked up when he saw her. Before zipping the flap closed she flung her wet socks out onto the grass. She could feel all the pebbles and sticks and the cold damp of the ground through her sleeping bag. Before they left Newfoundland, she and Kyle had stripped their beds and thrown all their blankets in the back of the car for the dog. Her schoolbooks were still locked in the empty house.

In the morning Shawna woke up stiff and unzipped the tent. The smell of woodsmoke was caught in her hair. No one else was up. She sat at the picnic table and watched the sun inch its way down the sides of the two strange mountains that cradled her.

Acknowledgements

Thank you to Sarah MacLachlan, Kelly Joseph, Amelia Spedaliere, Janie Yoon, Janice Zawerbny, and everyone at House of Anansi Press for their incredible generosity.

Thank you to Melanie Little for being such a thorough editor and teaching me so much about how to make a story work.

Thank you to Larry Mathews, Rob Finley, Jessica Grant, and Claire Wilkshire for their invaluable mentorship.

Thank you to Steve Crocker, Lisa Moore, Emily Amaral, Theo Crocker, Jess Gibson, Catherine Roberge, Alex Noel, Pretzel, and Poptart for their endless support.

EVA CROCKER's stories have been published in *Riddle Fence*, *The Overcast*, and the *Telegram*'s *Cuffer Anthology*. *Barrelling Forward* was shortlisted for the 2015 NLCU Fresh Fish Award for Emerging Writers. Crocker recently completed a master's degree in English Literature at Memorial University and received the University Medal for Excellence in Graduate Studies.